"The very talented Muriel Jensen has a definite skill for penning heartwarming, humorous tales destined to remain favorites...."

—*Romantic Times Magazine*

Dear Reader,

Here we are in Dancer's Beach again with Peg and Charlie, parents of the McKeon b̶_____ from the original WHO'S THE DA_____

Also at the b̶_____ Cliffside, a̶_____ They are Da̶_____ Bram Bishop_____ the CIA. They host a n̶_____ as the Three Musketeers an_____ paths with identical triplet sisters dressed as a Regency miss, a flapper and a Southern belle.

Seven months later one of the women is rescued from the Columbia River very pregnant and suffering from amnesia. But which of the three sisters is she? And the question everyone is asking is *who's the daddy?*

I hope you enjoy finding the answer!

Best wishes,

Muriel Jensen

**Watch for Muriel Jensen's next book
in the Who's the Daddy? series**

#866 FATHER FOUND available in March

Dear Reader,

Happy New Year! May this year bring you happiness, good health and all that you wish for. And at Harlequin American Romance, we're hoping to provide you with a year full of heartwarming books that you won't be able to resist.

Leading the month is *The Secretary Gets Her Man* by Mindy Neff, Harlequin American Romance's spin-off to Harlequin Intrigue's TEXAS CONFIDENTIAL continuity series. This exciting story focuses on the covert operation's much-mentioned wallflower secretary, Penny Archer.

Muriel Jensen's *Father Formula* continues her successful WHO'S THE DADDY? series about three identical sisters who cause three handsome bachelors no end of trouble when they discover one woman is about to become a mother. Next, after opening an heirloom hope chest, a bride-to-be suddenly cancels her wedding and starts having intimate dreams about a handsome stranger, in *Have Gown, Need Groom*. This is the first book of Rita Herron's new miniseries THE HARTWELL HOPE CHESTS. And Debbi Rawlins tells the emotional story of a reclusive rancher who opens his home—and his heart— to a lovely single mother, in *Loving a Lonesome Cowboy*.

In February, look for another installment in the RETURN TO TYLER series with *Prescription for Seduction* by Darlene Scalera.

Wishing you happy reading,

Melissa Jeglinski
Associate Senior Editor
Harlequin American Romance

MURIEL JENSEN
Father Formula

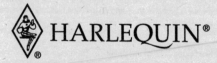

HARLEQUIN®

TORONTO • NEW YORK • LONDON
AMSTERDAM • PARIS • SYDNEY • HAMBURG
STOCKHOLM • ATHENS • TOKYO • MILAN • MADRID
PRAGUE • WARSAW • BUDAPEST • AUCKLAND

ISBN 0-373-16858-6

FATHER FORMULA

Copyright © 2001 by Muriel Jensen.

This edition published by arrangement with Harlequin Books S.A.

® and TM are trademarks of the publisher. Trademarks indicated with ® are registered in the United States Patent and Trademark Office, the Canadian Trade Marks Office and in other countries.

Visit us at www.eHarlequin.com

Printed in U.S.A.

ABOUT THE AUTHOR

Muriel Jensen and her husband, Ron, live in Astoria, Oregon, in an old four-square Victorian at the mouth of the Columbia River. They share their home with a golden retriever/golden Labrador mix named Amber, and five cats who moved in with them without an invitation. (Muriel insists that a plate of Friskies and a bowl of water are *not* an invitation!)

They also have three children and their families in their lives—a veritable crowd of the most interesting people and children. In addition, they have irreplaceable friends, wonderful neighbors and "a life they know they don't deserve but love desperately anyway."

Books by Muriel Jensen

HARLEQUIN AMERICAN ROMANCE

DANCER'S BEACH

15.
a. b. c. d. e. f.

Legend
1. Coast Groceries
2. Madsen's Nursery
3. Burgers by the Sea
4. Ocean View Motors
5. Homeowners' Hardware
6. Antiques
7. Kites & Treasures
8. D. B. Realty
9. Beanley's Furniture
10. Buckley Arms

11. City Park
  a. Library
  b. Playground
12. City Hall
13. Faith Community Church
14. Save Now Drugs

15. Bijou Theater
  a. Heads Up Salon
  b. McGinty's Photos
  c. Barbara's Boutique
  d. Veranda Videos
  e. Sew It Seams Fabrics
  f. Duane Ross Accounting
16. Detective Agency

17. Gifts
18. Sporting
      Goods
19. Bank

Beach

Bram's
Garage Apt

Cliffside
(David)

Trevyn's
Guest
House

Dancer Ave.

Beach Avenue

CLIFFSIDE

Beach

Chapter One

Alexis Ames reclined on her side on her sister Athena's bed, propped up on her elbow as she watched her fold clothing into a dark blue soft-sided bag. Athena, usually serious and sedate, placed a flowered bra and matching French-cut panties into the bag's front pocket.

"Now, there's something I never thought I'd see," Alexis said, pointing to the scraps of silk and lace as they were tucked away. "How will you be able to keep a straight face while addressing the jury, knowing you're wearing those?"

Athena blushed and laughed. "David bought them for me. And I won't be in court this trip."

Alexis was fascinated by her sister's blush. Athena had changed in a score of subtle little ways since taking up with David Hartford.

Athena practiced law in Washington, D.C., a champion of the oppressed and the underdog. She'd always been the serious one of the Ames triplets, every detail of her life organized for the best and most efficient outcome.

Of course, their aunt's sudden death in the crash
of a light plane in Hawaii had changed all their lives.
Athena had taken time off from her law practice,
Alexis had left her art studio in Rome, and Augusta
had arranged for a substitute teacher and had flown
in from northern California for the reading of Aunt
Sadie's will at the Portland, Oregon, office of her
attorney.

The news that Sadie had left Cliffside, her family's
home, to a mysterious beneficiary named David Hartford made all three sisters suspicious. Sadie had always promised the home to her nieces, and the will
offered no explanation for the sudden change in
plans.

When they'd learned that Hartford had already
taken possession of Cliffside and had rented the guest
house and the garage apartment to friends, Alexis and
her sisters had rented a car and driven to Dancer's
Beach on the Oregon Coast. They invited themselves
to a costume party the men were hosting in an attempt
to discover, through clever subterfuge, what they
didn't seem to be able to uncover with straightfor-
ward questions.

Only things had backfired. The men had been
dressed as the Three Musketeers, wigged and masked
and of similar height and coloring. Each sister had
attached herself to one of the men, the plan being that
she could use whatever means she deemed fit to
gather information.

When they'd met back at their car sometime later,
Athena had been the only one who still questioned
the men's sincerity. Then Alexis and her sisters had

resigned themselves to the situation and returned to their lives.

And then, just one brief week ago, Alexis had been visiting with friends at the American Club in Rome and seen a television broadcast about an unidentified young woman rescued from the Columbia River at Astoria, Oregon. The reporter said that a blow to the head had left her with amnesia.

Alexis gasped at the grainy image of the woman on a gurney being lifted into the back of an ambulance. It was one of her sisters. And she was very pregnant.

As she tried to assimilate that information she'd run closer to the television, hoping for a clue that would tell her which sister it was.

"When the victim's sister, Athena Ames, came with a friend to Astoria to claim her," the reporter went on, "the mystery woman had disappeared. She is five-seven, about 120 pounds, has long red hair, dark blue eyes, and may be looking for food or work since she had no purse and no identification on her when she was pulled from the river. She has now been missing eight days."

Alexis had stared in disbelief, then tried to call Athena, only to learn that she was on leave from the office for an indefinite period of time. Then she remembered that the news story had said "by the time her sister arrived—" and realized that she must be in Oregon. She called Patrick Connelly, a private detective who often worked for Athena, who gave her an address in Dancer's Beach.

Alexis had hung up the phone and stared at the

note she'd taken. Her sister was staying at the former home of their aunt. But where was the man who now owned the home?

She recalled that the news story had said, "by the time her sister and a *friend* had arrived—" Could it be...? She couldn't believe it.

But it was true.

When Athena and David Hartford met at the hospital, they'd decided to join forces in their search for Gusty, and had just decided to make the alliance permanent. Alexis and David's friend, Trevyn McGinty, had been their witnesses just two days ago in a simple service at Faith Community Church. Athena appeared to be hopelessly in love with David.

"Writers are temperamental, you know," Alexis said, referring to her new brother-in-law's current profession. With one sister missing, the other changed, and with the discovery that Aunt Sadie had left David the house because she, too, had been a CIA agent code-named "Auntie," Alexis was beginning to feel like a trespasser in someone else's life. "You're sure you're doing the right thing, closing up your D.C. office to open a law office in Dancer's Beach? I mean, you're used to big-city doings and important cases. What'll you find here to match that?"

Athena smiled. It was a scary look. Her usually intense sister actually appeared serene. "I've already found it," Athena replied. "And it far surpasses everything I've known so far."

Alexis would have found that nauseating if Athena hadn't been so sincere.

"What if this literary agent is wrong, and the publishers he wants David to meet don't consider him publishable after all?"

Athena shrugged. "Then he'll find another one. It's a good book. A great book."

Alexis leaned over the side of the bed to catch a folded pair of socks Athena had thrown at the suitcase and overshot. She tossed them back.

"So they really were CIA agents? *Our* Musketeers?"

Athena nodded as she closed the lid on the suitcase. "They really were. That's why it's such a great book. It's fiction, but it's based on everything David really knows."

Alexis sat up as Athena carried her suitcase to the door. "I'm sorry, but it's hard for me to imagine Trevyn McGinty as a CIA agent. Maybe as a cop in *Car 54, Where Are You?...*"

Athena gave her a scolding look over her shoulder as she pulled a lined raincoat out of the closet. "Lex, you're going to be here with him for at least a week helping with the boys while David's in New York and I close up my office. You have to buff up your attitude."

"He keeps making smart remarks to me."

"In response to your smart remarks." Athena grinned. "You're just upset because he got the better of you in that little altercation when you thought he'd broken in."

"Sure he did." Alexis avoided her sister's glance as she picked up her tote bag off the bed. "He's bigger and he didn't mind using his muscle."

"It was dark," Athena defended him. "He thought you were attacking him!"

Alexis had a clear memory of McGinty sprawled over her body on the kitchen floor as the frying pan she'd wielded flew through the air and crashed into the dishes on the drying rack. She remembered gasping for breath, certain her back would break.

She sighed dispiritedly. "To think I went to self-defense classes two nights a week for three months."

Athena laughed and opened the door. "I'm sure the training Uncle Sam gave him was more heavy-duty than your class at the Rome Y. You're sure you want us to leave the boys and the dog with you? Dotty will be gone until next Monday. You'll have to—" Athena grinned apologetically "—you know, remember to feed them, see that the boys get to school, walk the dog."

In acquiring David as her husband, Athena had also acquired the care of his two half brothers, Brandon, twelve, and Brady, ten. Alexis had known them just a matter of days, but she thought they were wonderful.

Equally wonderful was Ferdie, the boys' 110-pound Great Dane and Saint Bernard mix.

Alexis rolled her eyes at her. "I think I can handle that. I can't believe that you've turned from a warrior into some kind of Donna Reed and you still think of me as incompetent."

Athena turned to her, an aggressive tilt to her chin. "I do *not* think you're incompetent. It's just that, as an artist, you sometimes forget the normal, day-to-day things."

"Yeah, well, I'm not much of an artist at the moment." Alexis pushed her gently out the door. "And though I know your trip east isn't exactly for pleasure, I'm sure the two of you can use a little space after all you've been through since Gusty was pulled out of the water. And we can't even continue the search for her until Holden gets an answer on the passenger lists."

Brandon and Brady had confused Athena with a redheaded woman they'd seen at the Portland Airport while running away from their mother's home to stay with David. It had been the first time Gusty had been seen since she'd disappeared from the hospital.

Since then, Officer Holden of the Astoria Police, who'd been handling the investigation, had been checking the passenger lists for flights arriving at the baggage carousel where the boys had seen Gusty. It was a long and tedious process.

She'd been traveling with a man the boys had described as "scary looking," and the police were checking the identity of every passenger, presuming that they were probably traveling under assumed names, since Gusty reportedly no longer remembered hers.

Alexis wrapped her free arm around Athena's shoulders as they walked down the hallway to the stairs. "I'm sorry I wasn't around to help you the past couple of weeks."

Athena dismissed her apology with a shake of her head. "My only concern was that, when I couldn't locate you either, I wasn't sure which one of you they'd found."

Alexis made a scornful sound. "Like I'd ever turn up seven months pregnant."

Athena gave her a look Alexis found unsettling— as though she had knowledge Alexis didn't share. "Someday," she said with a curious little smile, "you'll meet the right man and wonder why you ever thought that." Then Athena squared her shoulders before going down the stairs. "The boys, the dog. Holden's number on the fridge. Is there anything I haven't covered?"

This efficiency was a glimpse of the old Athena and Alexis frankly considered it a relief.

"No, I'll take it from here. Don't worry about a thing. I'll look after everything and prod Holden every day for something to go on. You just enjoy the East Coast and your new husband. Maybe we'll even have Gusty here to welcome you back."

At the bottom of the stairs Athena wrapped her arms around her and for a moment they held each other fiercely, trying to make up for the gap Gusty's absence created in their lives.

"Yes," Athena said, composed again. "Try to make that happen. I'll call you from D.C." She picked up her bag and started out the door toward the car.

Alexis followed with her tote bag.

"And don't start any fights with Trevyn."

"He's the one who starts everything," Alexis argued.

"Yeah, right." Athena countered.

TREVYN MCGINTY HELPED his friend and landlord, David Hartford, pile luggage into the trunk of David's blue sedan. "Now, if you sell your book to these guys," Trevyn said, moving the toolbox and blankets aside to make room for David's brown leather bags, "what's the first thing you're supposed to demand in your contract?"

David handed him a fat briefcase. "That my portrait on the dust cover be taken by you."

Everything in place, Trevyn dusted off his hands and patted David on the back. "Very good. I'm glad I saved your life that time in Bangkok after all."

"As I recall, the idol I was hiding behind saved my life."

"Only because I arrived in time to return fire."

"You were three minutes late."

"And you're still here to continually remind me of that. Where's Bram, anyway? He can't still be in Mexico."

"He is. That wayward husband he was following loaded his SUV with pretty girls at the Barkley Regis and Bram followed him—into Mexico. He called me before he crossed the border. Some kind of big meeting going on, or something."

Bram Bishop had often been the third member of their CIA team, a security expert with more than twenty years experience. He'd retired with them almost ten months ago and had opened a detective agency in downtown Dancer's Beach. He lived in the apartment above Cliffside's four-car garage.

Trevyn frowned. "You think it's drugs? White slavers?"

"I don't know. I haven't heard from him since. I

tried to call him a couple of times when Gusty was first reported missing for some advice on where to start a search, but I couldn't get through on his cell phone.''

"How long's it been?"

"Three weeks."

Trevyn considered that, then dismissed it. "If it was anybody else, I'd worry."

"I know. He's fine." David grinned at him as Athena and Alexis walked out of the house toward them. The boys, shooting hoops on the edge of the driveway, stopped their game, shouldered their backpacks for school and fell in behind them, the dog loping along in step. "Are you going to be okay with Lex and the boys while Dotty's at her son's? Or should I arrange for a nanny and police protection?"

"Funny." Trevyn shoved him, then eyed the bags the women carried and reached into the trunk to re-arrange its cargo. "The boys are great. And Alexis has the house, I've got the guest house and if there's a just God, never the twain shall meet."

From what he'd learned so far, Trevyn guessed Alexis was the evil triplet. Though as beautiful as Athena with her long dark red hair and deep blue eyes, she had none of her courtesy. She was outspoken and outrageous—and she'd tried to bean him with a frying pan. It was hard to feel kindly toward a woman like that.

"What if Holden gets some news about Gusty?" David asked.

"I'll find her," Trevyn assured him, "without Lex's help."

"But she knows her better than you do," David argued, "even though you…"

Trevyn sighed impatiently at David's hesitation. "Even though I got Gusty pregnant. You can say it aloud. It isn't as though we don't all know she's seven and a half months along."

"You're *sure* you were with her?" David asked. "Considering how identical the girls are. I mean, with costumes and masks and just a brief glimpse of her face…"

"I made love to her," Trevyn said firmly, lowering his voice as the women approached. "She's the only sister who's pregnant. It was me."

"You're not going to go too nuts waiting around, are you?" David asked. "I know you'd like to try to find Gusty on your own, but I've got Wren still looking for her and I'll feel so much better knowing you're here with Lex and the boys."

Wren was an old friend of theirs from their "company" days who'd also retired and now freelanced his spook skills.

Trevyn would have preferred action, but he owed David a lot. When they weren't on "company" business, he and David had worked together at the Chicago Tribune, David as a journalist, Trevyn as a photojournalist. He nodded. "I'm fine with it, and I'll keep my eye on the boys. If Alexis inadvertently disappears…"

"Trev—"

"Okay, okay. I'll watch out for her, too."

"Thanks for making it all fit, Trevyn." Athena beamed at him as he tucked her two bags into a tight spot. "If we'd left this to David, he'd have made me leave most of my stuff."

"Oh, he's always been selfish," Trevyn teased, then closed the trunk and David locked it. "You must see something in him that's invisible to the rest of us. There. You're all set."

Athena hugged each of the boys, promising that they would call, and asking what they wanted in the way of souvenirs from Washington and New York.

"A New York Yankees hat," Brandon said, reaching up as David hugged him. He was fair-haired and spindly and very, very smart.

Brady stood back, arms folded, an uncharacteristic pout on his dark-featured face. Trevyn had spent time with the boys when they'd visited David over the past few years, and he'd never seen Brady anything but hopelessly cheerful. Trevyn suspected he was upset about David's trip.

"When are you coming back?" Brady asked, still keeping his distance.

Trevyn noticed that David didn't move in. He admired that about his friend. In the field, he'd always waited for the right moment.

"About a week, maybe ten days," David replied.

"You're sure."

"I'm sure."

"'Cause if it's any longer, you'll miss Parents' Night. You get to see all my work and look at my classroom. And there's cookies."

"We won't miss it. I promise. Athena put the flyer on the fridge."

Brady eyed David.

Alexis and Athena suddenly made a production of getting Athena into the car, pretending not to notice it had become a tense guy moment.

Brandon elbowed Brady. "Don't be a doofus," he said under his breath.

Brady gave him a lethal look, then wrapped his arms around David's middle. "Okay," he said. "Have a good time."

David held him, then drew him away and looked down into his face. "Tell me what's on your mind," he said.

Brady's lips parted and there was an instant of silence, then he said quietly, "I was just worried about Parents' Night at school. There's goodies, you know. And you get to look in my classroom."

"We'll be back in time," David assured him, then put an arm around him and led him toward the driver's side of the car. At the door, he stopped and asked, frankly, "Brady, are you worried that your mom will send Darby after you guys again?"

David had told Trevyn that Darby was their mother's new husband and the reason for their leaving home when he'd put Ferdie in the pound.

Brady folded his arms again. "I worry about that sometimes," he admitted.

David leaned against the car door and put his hands on Brady's shoulders. "Mom signed papers that make me your legal guardian, remember? They're in our safety-deposit box. I showed them to you."

Brady nodded. "I know."

"Then, there's nothing to worry about."

"Yeah." Brady forced a smile but it was unconvincing.

David looked up at Trevyn. "Your Uncle Trev isn't going to let anyone take you away, or let anything happen to you while I'm gone. Right, Trev?"

Trevyn stepped forward with a shrug. "Well, unless it's a tribe of beautiful babes, or something, and they want me, too, then of course..."

Brandon barked a laugh and Brady smiled despite himself.

David glared at Trevyn.

"No one takes them," Trevyn said dutifully, pulling Brady into the crook of his arm, "and nothing hurts them. Got it." He caught Brandon in his other arm and drew him back from the car. "Don't worry about a thing."

"Easier said than done by anyone who knows you," David countered, opening the car door.

"I'm here to straighten out whatever he messes up," Alexis said, coming around the car to give David a hug. "You take care of my sister, buddy, or you answer to me."

She closed the car door as David climbed in behind the wheel.

FERDIE BARKED and tried to follow the car as it pulled away, but Brandon held him back by the collar.

Alexis stared until the car was out of sight, feeling more alone than she'd felt in a long time. Gusty was missing and Athena wasn't really part of the triumvirate anymore. She had another life now.

And this was the story of *her* life, Alexis thought—never quite part of the group. Different. Lonely.

"Aren't these guys going to be late for school?"

Trevyn's voice interrupted her thoughts and reminded her that she wasn't alone at all. Lonely, maybe, but hardly alone.

He was tall and broad, dark hair ruffling a little in the afternoon breeze, eyes inky black and taunting. If he was anyone else, she'd admit that he was gorgeous. But he wasn't. He was the man who'd dropped her effortlessly to the kitchen floor and knelt astride her.

"I know the schedule, thank you," she replied politely, then turned her attention to Brandon and Brady. "Do you want me to walk you to the bus stop?"

The boys looked at each other in horror.

She realized immediately that had been a faux pas.

Brandon looked hopefully at Trevyn. "Can you take us in the truck?"

"Sure." Trevyn dug his keys out of his pocket as the boys raced into the open garage. Alexis caught Ferdie's collar to prevent him from following.

Trevyn smiled at Alexis. "Don't take it to heart. Being delivered in a truck looks better to your buddies than walking with a woman in tow. I'll be back in a few minutes."

Alexis sighed as she watched them all climb into the truck. Ruled by testosterone at ten and twelve. What a world.

They waved to her as the truck disappeared down the drive. Ferdie whined mournfully.

She walked toward the bushes that surrounded the headland rather than going back to the house, slapping her thigh in an invitation for the dog to follow. She felt edgy and strange here without her sisters. She'd lived much of her adult life without them, but when they were here at Cliffside, they were usually together.

From behind the width of the hedge, she took in the breathtaking view of bright blue sky meeting even bluer water. She closed her eyes and drew in a deep whiff of the salty fresh air. She felt it fill her body and bring back memories of her, Athena and Augusta as children playing like wild things on this lawn.

She'd had dark and selfish thoughts then, she recalled. She used to think that her mother would love her if she could just get rid of the competition. Athena was so competent and Gusty was so charming and agreeable. Alexis, unfortunately, had a gift for candor and a talent for art, neither of which was appreciated by their mother.

In her hopeful, positive moments, the young Alexis was very grateful for her sisters, realizing how bleak her life would be without them. With their mother ignoring them and wanting to claim the limelight herself, and their father taking every opportunity he could to stay away, all they had was one another and the trips to Aunt Sadie's in Dancer's Beach.

But when she felt hurt and resentful, she imagined life without Athena and Gusty. She pretended they had never been, and that it was just her, hand in hand with her mother.

There would be no delighted stares of passersby

fascinated by three red-haired little girls dressed alike, or in three shades of the same color. No one would stop and tell her mother how beautiful her children were, how much they looked like her.

It would just be the two of them. No one would notice. They would just go shopping together and with no one else to claim her mother's attention, Alexis would have it all. Her mother would look at her and smile.

She'd seen other mothers do that to their children. They didn't even have to say anything. Love filled their eyes, made their smiles glow, brought about a ruffle of the child's hair or a sudden hug.

Alexis had always waited for such a moment, but it never came.

By the time she was a teenager, she'd resigned herself to her fate and allied herself with her sisters in their struggle to find personal value and self-esteem.

Athena found it in an ability to argue clearly with anyone about anything. It was soon obvious she was headed for law school.

Augusta loved knowledge and children, and glowed when she talked about becoming a teacher.

Alexis decided to parlay her art into a life. Art, she'd learned early on, could never be simply a career.

Her talent won her a year's study abroad in college, and she decided to remain there afterward, loving the daily contact with paintings, sculptures and buildings that had been created by Michelangelo, da Vinci, and all the other names associated with the Renaissance.

And, truth be told, it allowed her to run away. She didn't have to watch her sisters, so sure what they wanted to do, so secure in their abilities to do it, while she floundered with a skill that was unpredictable at best.

She appreciated being able to launch her efforts thousands of miles from anyone who knew her.

She'd achieved a fair measure of success, was well accepted by the art community in Rome, and sold very well at the small but prestigious gallery that represented her in New York City.

That was far more than most artists enjoyed, Alexis reminded herself as she started back toward the house, determined to find something productive to do. She would have to prepare dinner tonight. With her limited culinary skills, that should take her most of the day to plan and prepare.

She'd just reached the driveway when Trevyn's truck came rumbling and gasping up the hill. He drew up beside her, stopped and leaped out of the truck.

"Did you beat the bus?" she asked.

"Got there in the nick of time. Did Athena or Dave tell you how to call me from the house if you need anything?"

Alexis now enjoyed a fragile but determined sense of self that was sometimes manifested in the need to be more clever and more right than whomever she dealt with. Trevyn McGinty, however, didn't seem to understand her need to be superior.

"Thank you," she said politely with a quick glance at him. She wasn't sure why, but it made her uncomfortable to look at him too long. His eyes said he knew she was a phoney. He couldn't know, of course. She attributed that feeling to her worry about Gusty, and the weirdness of their situation. Everything seemed foreign and threatening. "But I'm not worried, and I doubt that I'll need to call you."

The cool reply was intended to put him off.

It failed. He grinned, hands in the pockets of a dark blue fleece jacket. "What if you get up in the early morning to make tea," he asked with feigned innocence, "and surprise another intruder?"

She'd come out without a jacket and rubbed her arms in the thin green knit of a light sweater. Annoyance bubbled out of her politeness. "You find it impossible to be a gentleman about that, don't you?"

He shrugged a shoulder. "Only because you refuse to admit that I had every right to be there."

"You were using a lock pick!" Her voice was rising. "Why didn't you knock on the door like a normal person?"

"It was four-fifteen in the morning," he replied. "Why weren't you asleep like a normal person?"

"I was…" She'd begun to answer instinctively, then thought better of it. She'd been worried about her sister, worried about her art, worried about being twenty-nine and feeling no closer to an answer to what her life was all about. Art, certainly, but that left her pretty one-dimensional.

"I was thinking," she finally said. "I know you'd just returned from Canada, but couldn't you have sat in your car for a couple of hours and waited for a sign that someone was awake?"

The amusement left his eyes. "I'd just seen the

news about Gusty. I needed information. I knew Dave
wouldn't mind if I let myself in.''

She could allow him that, she decided grudgingly,
even if he had been foolish enough to make love to
her sister on a few hours' acquaintance. But she still
wasn't feeling friendly.

"What kind of person travels with a lock pick,
anyway?''

"A former spook. I was always better at it than
Dave or Bram, so I carried the pick.''

"Well, in the world of non-spooks, it's a question-
able talent.''

"Sorry. Force of habit. And I didn't expect the
house to be occupied by anyone but Dave, except
maybe Dotty. How was I to know he'd picked up
four other people?''

"I'd have thought the spy business would teach
you to never assume anything.''

Something shifted in his eyes for an instant and
she caught a glimpse of old pain.

"Yeah, well, I'm trying to unlearn a lot of old
habits from those days.'' He looked away for a moment, as though he realized he'd betrayed something
personal. When his eyes settled on her again, they
were self-deprecating. "The work teaches you to trust
nothing and no one, to believe only what you see,
and only if you've seen it from the beginning. Like
lock picking, those qualities don't help the transition
to normal life.''

He leaned down to ruffle the dog's ears, then
pointed in the direction of the guest house he occupied. It looked very much like the two-story brick

Colonial Revival that was Cliffside. It also had two stories, but only two windows across instead of four, and no attic gables.

It was surrounded on the back and sides by fir trees interspersed with mountain ash that were now alive with bright red berries. Soon they would attract clouds of little birds.

"I've got work to do," he said, seemingly anxious suddenly to escape her. "If you do need anything, press the com line, then 2."

"Thank you." She tried to sound brisk and not too sincere.

He climbed back into the truck and pulled into the garage.

Ferdie loped after the truck, barking, but Alexis called him back. He returned dutifully and she leaned down to kiss his big snout. "You don't need him," she assured the dog quietly, aware that the wind might carry her voice. "I'm going to feed you well and take you for walks, and we're going to keep each other company."

Ferdie followed her to the big house, but looked longingly in Trevyn's direction.

Alexis took hold of the old front door handle, depressed the thumb plate and pulled—and nothing happened. She stared at the locked door in surprise for an instant, then smiled reassuringly at the dog as she remembered that Athena had given her a key.

She reached into the pocket of her green-and-brown-plaid slacks and met empty fabric. The key, she remembered, was on her dresser.

"Well, damn," she told the dog with a sigh. "I'm going to need McGinty after all."

Chapter Two

Fine, Trevyn thought as he carefully packed bulbs and reflectors into a padded cardboard box. He'd been a fool to offer to help her anyway. She was as different from what he remembered of Gusty as a negative was from a print. It had the same image but everything else about it was different.

The woman he'd danced with the night of the costume party had been warm and funny and had looked into his eyes with a sweetness that had been missing in his life since dark memories had taken over. His mother had had it, but she'd died when he was in high school. The women he'd met in college and since had been smart, ambitious, witty and equal to anything.

He'd appreciated them, but he hadn't realized how appealing gentle laughter had been until he'd heard it, how completely mind-blowing it was to have a woman walk into his arms and lean her weight into him with a trust that was more instinctive than learned. Something in her had responded to something in him without any real knowledge of him.

They'd talked about nothing important. The eye appeal of Dancer's Beach, chocolate-covered cherries, the White Sox, Cliffside.

He smiled with the new knowledge that her interest in the house had been part of the plan she and her sisters had concocted to find out why their aunt had left Cliffside to David. It amused him to think that when she'd met him, she'd considered him a criminal.

He should be offended, he supposed, but considering her complete capitulation before the night was over—and the fact that it had resulted in his becoming a father—it was hard to put a bad spin on it.

Anxiety and impatience tried to force themselves into the forefront of his mind when he thought of her helpless and alone—except for the scary guy with whom the boys had reported seeing her at the airport when they'd run away. No one knew whether he was a threat or a friend—and Trevyn couldn't think about him as the former or he'd go insane.

He'd called Officer Holden this morning and learned only that the verification of passengers whose luggage had gone through that particular carousel was ongoing and, so far, everyone checked out.

Trevyn continued packing, something comforting in the handling of long-used equipment. There was nothing to do but wait.

In the meantime, he would see what he'd gotten on the rolls of film he'd shot in Canada, then he'd concentrate on getting his studio ready in town. Photography was a high-maintenance mistress.

He was just about to lock himself in the darkroom

when he heard the lion's head knocker pound twice against the door. He hurried through the kitchen and the living room, wondering if Dave and Athena had forgotten something.

It was Alexis, Ferdie sitting beside her. Her arms were folded and her chin was angled defensively.

She needed something—already. He tried not to betray his enjoyment in the fact.

He reached a hand out to the dog, who snuffled then licked it. "Yes?" Trevyn asked.

"I left my key on the dresser," she said lightly, trying to convince him that she wasn't at all uncomfortable in approaching him. "And the door locked behind me when I carried out Athena's bag."

"Oh." He nodded sympathetically.

She waited for more.

This was just too good.

She drew a breath, her patience clearly strained. She asked courteously, "May I borrow yours?"

He spread his hands helplessly. "I don't have one."

"What do you mean, you don't have one?" she demanded. Realizing her voice had risen, she lowered it and added reasonably, "When you picked the lock, I thought you said you'd only misplaced your key."

"I had," he replied, "and when I found it, I gave it to Athena. I imagine that's the one she gave you. Have you tried the windows?"

She was beginning to realize he was playing her like a violin. Her gaze was condemning. "You and David put the storm windows in yesterday."

He snapped his fingers. "That's right! I forgot."

She told him with her eyes what she wanted.

He gave her a look that told her she was going to have to ask for it aloud.

She shifted her weight, threatened him with a fulminating glare that bounced right off him, then closed her eyes and expelled a deep breath.

"Would you, please," she asked, emphasizing the *please,* "pick the lock for me?"

Yes. That did feel as good as he'd imagined it would. But she was Gusty's sister, after all, and he was, despite her contention, a gentleman.

"I'd be happy to," he said amiably.

HE HAD THE DOOR OPEN in a matter of seconds.

Alexis forced a grateful smile. "Thank you very much. I appreciate your help."

He inclined his head as he pocketed the pick. "I meant it when I offered it earlier. We're probably going to be in-laws, after all."

"Really." She tried to imagine her sweet, gentle sister married to this smart-mouthed man and couldn't quite see it. But she was carrying his baby.

It was on the tip of her tongue to invite him in for coffee, but it was too hard to make the concession.

"I'm going to town in the morning, if you need anything," he said. "You can come along or just give me a list."

"Thank you, but I thought walking to town would be a good way for both Ferdie and me to get our exercise. I promised that I'd see he got his walks."

Trevyn nodded. "All right. Well, I've got to get back to work."

"Thanks again."

"Sure."

Alexis closed the door behind him, then parted the drapes to watch him walk away. For all his personality problems, she thought, watching the easy movement of tight, lean hips, he had few physical ones.

Disgusted with herself for noticing, she closed the drapes, then spent the afternoon being domestic.

She put a load of laundry in the wash, checked the contents of the kitchen cupboards so that she could pick up what she needed on tomorrow's walk. She discovered a decided lack of chocolate, pastry and peanuts.

Dotty was an excellent cook who provided good home-style healthy meals. While Alexis appreciated that, she knew that left to her own devices, she would eat mostly what didn't have to be cooked and could be carried around in her hand. Of course, she had to find something for the boys to eat for dinner.

Then inspiration struck. She would take them for hamburgers or for pizza! She couldn't do that every night, but a small adventure tonight would help them get acquainted.

She put her clothes in the dryer, then took Ferdie out into the yard for a game of fetch. He played eagerly.

The wind picked up and Alexis decided to add a jacket to her shopping list tomorrow. Sunny Italy didn't require one, but fall in cool, rainy Oregon would.

The scent of pine and salt air brought back tumbled memories of her childhood, though, and she stopped a moment to inhale. She remembered picnics with Aunt Sadie on the beach, Alexis and her sisters playing with their dolls in the front yard, and when that grew tiresome, climbing trees and playing hide-and-seek in the woods behind the house.

She'd always tired first of the playing-house games, though Gusty could have fed and diapered her dolls forever. Alexis and Athena would eventually escape her scenarios of adult sisters in suburbia having babies and dinner parties and run to the woods for more physical exercise.

Gusty would eventually join them when she grew lonely, but she didn't enjoy running and climbing like her sisters did.

Alexis experienced a paralyzing pang of desperation. Where *was* she? What had happened to her? And who was the "scary-looking man" Brandon and Brady had seen with her at the airport?

Unable to pursue that thought without going crazy, Alexis called Ferdie to her and went back into the house. She filled the dog's bowl, gave him fresh water, then went to check on her laundry.

She folded it, then carried it upstairs and placed it on the dresser. She had the room Athena had occupied before she moved in with David. The bed and the dresser were different, but she enjoyed the familiar sight of the Mickey Mouse alarm clock on the bedside table.

She opened the sketchbook she'd brought with her from Rome and looked through all the studies of faces she'd done on the plane. Since she'd arrived, she'd done sketches of the boys, both reaching up to dunk the ball in the basket, and several of Ferdie running, sleeping, leaping in the air for a Frisbee.

The work was skillful, but she knew when it came to putting paint to canvas, she would be devoid of ideas, lacking in inspiration and, after three long months of that, without the will to try.

She would have wallowed in self-pity, but she'd taught herself to combat this mood over the past year. All she had to do was remember the artists she revered. Michelangelo, who painted the ceiling of the Sistine Chapel while lying on his back on scaffolding over a period of four years; Matisse, who painted by attaching his brush to a long stick when he was too old and ill to get out of bed; the contemporary Chuck Close, who was paralyzed and used a forklift to raise himself to work on his huge portraits and had a device attached to his hand to allow him to paint.

A slump was hardly the same as an infirmity. She would recover from this, if she could just figure out what had caused it in the first place.

In the meantime, she had to keep working.

She called one of her studio partners in Rome and asked him to mail the large wooden box in which she kept all her paints, the jar that held her brushes, her roll of canvas.

"*Bella!*" he exclaimed worriedly. "You are not coming home?"

"Not for a while, Claudio." She wanted to tell him that this was home, but he was just twenty and he'd known her only in Rome. He wouldn't understand. "I'm sending you money to cover the postage."

"Money? What is money?" he demanded. "The studio is cold without you, Lexia."

She smiled at his impassioned voice. She thought he had the potential to be a fine artist, but so far he had more emotion than skill. Still, skill could be learned and emotion couldn't, so things were in his favor.

"Don't try to charm me, Claudio," she teased. Flirting was second nature to him. "We both know you're in love with Giulia."

"Giulia," he said, his rich accent putting scorn into the name, "has gone to Palermo with Ponti. My heart is a stone. It beats no more."

"Oh, Claudio." She was sure he was heartbroken. He and the vintner's beautiful daughter had been friends since they were children, and Claudio's adopted father had worked for Giulia's. Their romance had blossomed only a year ago, just before she went to spend six months with relatives in New York. When she returned, Ponti, the son of a famous Italian designer had pursued her relentlessly. He'd also been a childhood friend who'd noticed her beauty and maturity when she'd returned home. "I'm sorry. I thought she'd have more sense."

"The whole world is mad," he declared, then added with theatrical tragedy, "and I am alone."

"Well, now's your chance to make a date with that pretty little waitress at the trattoria. You've always admired her."

He sighed. "I pine for you," he said, "and you send me to other women."

"I'm too old for you, Claudio," she said practically. "How many times do I have to tell you that?"

"What is age, *bella*," he asked, "when the heart yearns?"

She smiled to herself. She should be lucky enough to find a man closer to her own age who was this persistent. "Then consider the fact that I'm almost six thousand miles away, my friend. You may dismiss age, but distance must be dealt with. Now, go ask that pretty waitress for a date tonight and stop this foolishness. Let me know how it goes. And don't forget to send my paints and brushes."

"You wound me." He was silent a moment. "Very well, I will send your things. But when the night is quiet, you will hear my heart beating for you, no matter how great the distance."

"Unless Giulia comes back to you," she taunted.

"You are a devil woman," he accused, a smile in his voice.

"Goodbye, Claudio."

"Goodbye, *bella*."

Alexis hung up the phone, longing for her fourth-floor studio in the heart of the noisy, busy city. But only for a moment. She remembered quickly the frustration she'd felt there the past year, and though she'd been very upset about her missing sister, she'd also been grateful for an excuse to come home.

She turned in the direction of a soft whine just in time to see Ferdie burst from the room and race downstairs. She heard excited barking as the front door opened and closed and the boys' voices returned his greetings.

Alexis went downstairs to welcome them home and found them already in the kitchen, rooting through the freezer. They emerged with softball-sized blueberry muffins.

She watched Brandon wrap his in a paper towel and place it in the microwave with obvious experience. Then he nuked Brady's muffin while his brother retrieved two cans of pop and the butter from the refrigerator.

"How'd everything go today?" she asked.

Both boys looked up with smiles then returned to the serious task of "filleting" the muffins into thin slices that allowed more buttering surfaces.

"Good," Brandon replied.

"Yeah," Brady agreed.

"I thought we'd go for pizza tonight," she said, wondering if they'd have room for it after that muffin. "Or burgers if you'd like that better."

Brandon was already chewing the first slice as he buttered the last. He swallowed and said, "Cool."

Brady picked up his stacked plate and pop can and asked hopefully, "Can we watch TV?"

She smiled. David had coached her on this. "Until five o'clock, then you have to do your homework. I thought we'd go to dinner about six."

"Okay." Brady was already past her and on his way to the family room. Brandon put the butter back into the refrigerator, wiped the counter clean of crumbs, then turned to Alexis before closing the refrigerator door. "Did you want something to eat?"

She hadn't spent much time with children the boys'

ages, but she didn't think tidying up after themselves was usual behavior.

"No, thanks," she replied. "And thank you for cleaning up."

"You're welcome." Brandon followed in Brady's wake.

Alexis watched him go and wondered how they'd achieved such confidence and competence. Athena had told her a little about their wealthy mother, who went from one husband to another, having children in an attempt to hold them to her then ultimately losing them anyway.

A careless mother had left Alexis feeling inadequate and adrift.

She tried to remember if she'd had confidence at that age. No, she'd been reckless and wild, but that had been intended to conceal the fear that she had no value.

Her art had helped give her a sense of self. Getting back to it again was the only solution. It would be painful to see inadequate work take shape, but it would consume her while the boys were at school and that would help her maintain her sanity, such as it was.

She would buy a disposable camera tomorrow and photograph parts of downtown Dancer's Beach. There was beautiful scenery, buildings with interesting architectural detail, streets lined with park benches and old-fashioned streetlights.

Perhaps she could capture the heart of small-town life that was disappearing all across America.

Schmaltzy idea as paintings went, but it was a place to start.

BRANDON AND BRADY SPRINKLED a jumbo three-meat pizza with red pepper flakes and Parmesan cheese and ate the entire thing, going back twice for refills at the salad bar.

She allowed them three turns each on a video game car chase, then drove home, stopping for a carton of ice cream along the way.

When they arrived home, there was a message from David and Athena saying that they'd arrived in New York and were staying at the Plaza. They had left the number.

"Let's call them!" Brady suggested eagerly.

Alexis glanced at the clock. "Brady, it's well after eleven in New York. They're probably fast asleep."

"Maybe not."

"We'll call tomorrow when you come home from school."

"Maybe they're not asleep," Brady insisted. "Dave works late lots of times."

"But he's married now, doofus," Brandon said, heading for the stairs.

"So?" Brady demanded.

"So, they're probably...you know." Brandon cast a knowing but embarrassed glance in Alexis's direction and waved a hand to replace the words he couldn't quite say.

"What?" Brady insisted.

Alexis opened her mouth to suggest a diplomatic explanation when Brady's eyes suddenly widened and his expression made it clear that he understood. He looked horrified for a moment, then shoved Brandon aside and ran up the stairs.

Brandon heaved a long-suffering sigh and shook his head. "He's still kind of young," he said, and followed him, Ferdie trailing behind.

Alexis was stunned by that reaction. She knew that children Brady's age discussed sex among themselves, but often hated the suggestion that their parents or guardians practiced it.

But she was fairly sure that hadn't been disgust on Brady's face, but fear. She didn't understand what that meant. Judging by his behavior with Athena, he seemed to adore her.

"Let me know," she called after Brandon, "before you turn the lights out."

When Brandon called shortly after nine, Brady's room was already dark. Alexis tucked Brandon in, then patted the dog lying on a blanket across the boy's feet.

"French toast for breakfast?" Alexis asked before flipping off the light.

"Just cereal, please," he said, snuggling into his pillow. "We've got Graham O's."

"And you don't trust my cooking?"

He laughed. "Nope. Good night."

"Good night, Brandon."

She went across the hall to Brady's room, braved the quiet darkness and looked down on him. She suspected he simply pretended to be asleep, but she tucked his blankets in anyway, then went to the door.

"*I'd* like French toast," a voice said in the darkness.

Relieved to have some response from him, though still worried about his unusual behavior, Alexis replied briefly, "You got it. Should I get you up a little early so you'll have more time?"

"More time?"

"To spread butter and drizzle syrup. You have to cover all the corners, you know, or it isn't as good."

"Yeah," he said. "That's true."

"Brady?" she blurted, moving surreptitiously back toward the bed. "Are you worried about something?"

Silence.

"Because if you are," she went on intrepidly, "you can tell me and I'll do what I can to help. I know I'm not as good as having David and Athena here, but I'm sort of like your aunt now. So you can tell me if you're worried. Or afraid."

There was silence for another moment, then he said finally, "No. Nothing."

"Okay." Dispiritedly she reversed directions. "Two pieces or three?"

"Three."

"Good night, Brady."

"Night," he replied.

All right, she told herself as she walked down the stairs to look through the kitchen and make sure they did indeed have syrup. She hadn't exactly conquered Everest, but she'd given Brady something to look forward to in the morning. And that might help the curious fear he seemed to be dealing with.

She was relieved beyond words to find a bottle of syrup on a shelf in the refrigerator door.

Chapter Three

Trevyn had the nightmare again. Something told him Farah would try to come along on the raid on the campsite despite his insistence that she shouldn't. The feeling had swelled inside him until fear began to permeate the calm, deadly edge that was so important to his work.

He'd expected to find her at the head of the trail that led to the campsite, but she wasn't there. He wanted to take that as a good sign, but he couldn't. His brain and his body refused to relax.

He discovered only moments later that she'd gone ahead of them in some misguided plan to clear the way for them, and that her traitorous brother had warned the camp.

He heard the gunfire, heard her scream.

Then he heard himself scream.

There was gunfire from three directions as he ran toward her. She was dead. He knew that before he reached her. And as he knelt there, staring at her stillness, he felt that he was dead, too.

But he and Bram and Dave were pinned down by

loud, continuous bursts of gunfire, and he had an overpowering need to stop it, to stop all sound so that he could think.

Dave took hold of his arm and was pulling him backward.

He resisted. He couldn't leave Farah. Maybe he'd been wrong. He wasn't a doctor, after all. Maybe she was still alive.

He struggled against Dave, who finally helped him lift her body onto his shoulder, then knelt with Bram to cover his escape.

Trevyn awoke in a cold sweat, panic and grief at the very edge of his consciousness, the darkness he lived with all the time threatening to suffocate him.

Then he noticed the familiar beige wallpaper with little flecks of brown in it, and the chair in the corner over which he'd thrown his shirt and jeans. No camouflage, no flack jacket. He was back in Chicago.

No, he reminded himself, spotting the photo he'd taken of a lone freighter in the middle of the vast ocean just beyond the edge of Cliffside's property. He was in Dancer's Beach. He was starting over. He was opening a portrait studio.

He'd thought he'd seen the end of the nightmares, the occasional confusion about the past, but apparently he had more work to do on that. That was fine. Mostly, he had it together.

Everything began to settle down inside him. Until he remembered that he was going to be a father. Then he sat up, feeling excitement and trepidation all at once. How could a man in darkness raise a baby?

He liked babies, he told himself. He'd photographed a lot of them in his time at the *Tribune*—in good situations and in bad—and he'd been touched every time by both their fragility and their miraculous endurance.

He prayed that Gusty had endurance. He knew so little about her, except that on the night of the costume party, she'd walked into his arms like a beautiful bundle of everything he'd needed at that moment.

He had to take care of her.

He had to be with her when their baby was born, whatever bad memories he had. They were his responsibility.

But at the rate the search for her was going, their baby would be a toddler before he saw her again. For a man accustomed to taking action, having to wait was frustrating, exasperating, and downright infuriating.

Still, those were emotions he'd grown familiar with in his journey to reclaim his life since Afghanistan. He knew that the only way to fight it was to take action in whatever avenue was open to him.

He climbed out of bed and jumped into the shower. He'd rented his studio before he'd left for Canada, but there'd been little time to work on it. It had been cleaned but needed paint, furniture, signs, and he had to move in his equipment.

He wondered idly as he dressed if he should ask Alexis if there was anything she needed. She'd insisted yesterday morning that she didn't think she'd ever need help from him—then she'd come over, pride in hand, when she'd found herself locked out.

He let himself enjoy that memory for a moment, then grabbed his jacket and checked his watch. The boys would be waiting for the bus already. He headed out to the truck.

The issue of whether or not to approach her was settled for him when she walked right by him, Ferdie prancing excitedly on the end of a long leash.

"Good morning," she called, her arm stretched way out, thanks to the dog's eagerness. "We're off for our constitutional." Then she did an almost theatrical double take, and dragged the dog to a stop, frowning as she focused on Trevyn. "Is everything all right?"

The dream always lingered in his eyes for a while. He hated that, considered it a vulnerability, a weakness. After their mild confrontation yesterday, he was surprised by her concern, and annoyed by it.

"Sure," he replied. "Why wouldn't it be?"

"Because you look a little…" She paused, apparently searching for the right word. There couldn't be one, as far as he was concerned.

She must have read that in his eyes. She shook her head as the dog tugged on her, extending her arm as though she were on the rack. "My mistake," she said, giving him the feeling she knew she was letting him get away with something.

That annoyed him further.

"Need anything from town?" he shouted as she picked up speed in the wake of the dog. He did it to prove to himself that she might annoy him but she couldn't upset him.

"No, thanks!" she replied over her shoulder as

Ferdie kept going. They raced toward the tree-lined driveway.

Trevyn opened the four-car garage. David's spot was empty, but Bram's Jeep was in place, looking none the worse for the fact that Athena had dumped it on its side on her way to town when she'd first arrived in Dancer's Beach.

David had had it towed and repaired.

Trevyn climbed into his battered red truck. He should get something else someday, he thought. A neat van or SUV onto which he could fasten magnetic signs with the name of his studio. Once he decided on a name.

Hot Shots? Picture Perfect? Or the more formal McGinty Photos, or Trevyn McGinty Photography?

Nothing struck a chord.

He drove off toward town, honking at Alexis and Ferdie at the bottom of the driveway, offering a brief wave.

She waved back, smiling.

That was how he remembered Gusty looking the last time he saw her.

ALEXIS AND FERDIE RAN through the park in downtown Dancer's Beach. After the dog had worked off steam—though how he could still have any after the mile and a half walk to town was beyond her—they walked up and down the main street and several side streets. She took photographs of scenes she might paint—children on swings in the park, three older men on a bench under a streetlight, kibitzing as the world went by, two little old ladies looking in the window of a flower shop, the old hotel.

The Buckley Arms was a turn-of-the-century gray-and-white building, five stories high, with an old-fashioned awning to shelter those waiting for cabs in the rain. She smiled, wondering how often people who rode cabs visited Dancer's Beach.

She took several shots, then noticed that the coffee bar on the bottom floor of the hotel was still there. She tied Ferdie to a newspaper stand in the front, then went inside to order a hazelnut latte.

She was considering a hazelnut biscotti to go with it when a voice called from behind her, "Athena!"

Alexis had been accustomed to being mistaken for one or the other of her sisters when they were children, but they'd been apart so much as adults that it hadn't happened in years.

She turned around in surprise, to find an older couple at a round table, half-finished cups of coffee and the newspaper between them.

The woman clearly waited for recognition. "Peg McKeon?" She smiled expectantly, putting a hand on the man's arm. "Charlie? We were in the antique shop when you were looking for an egg whip for your sister."

Alexis went to their table, smiling apologetically. "I'm Alexis," she explained. "We're identical."

Peg continued to smile. "So, *you're* the one she was shopping for!"

Alexis shook her head. "That's Augusta. We're triplets."

Peg put a hand to her lips in amazement. "My goodness! I'd have sworn…!"

The man stood and pulled a third chair back. "I've always thought there should be a system for making copies of pretty girls. If you're not meeting someone, would you like to join us?"

The name McKeon was ringing a bell in Alexis's memory. "Well, sure, if I'm not imposing."

"Of course not. I'll get your drink."

Before Alexis could tell him she hadn't paid for it yet, he had and was delivering it, along with the cookie. "I saw you eyeing the biscotti," he said as he put it down in front of her. "Impulses should always be indulged. Where's Athena these days?"

"Thank you, Charlie. She's in New York." She broke her cookie in half and dunked the end in the latte. "Her new husband is meeting with an agent about a book deal, and then she's closing up her law office in D.C. to move here."

Peg nodded knowingly. "So, she did find love."

When Alexis looked surprised that her sister would have spoken to strangers on such a subject, Peg added, "I'd been telling her that our sons have all found wonderful wives, but we were worried about our daughter, who doesn't seem to be able to hold a relationship together. Athena told me not to worry, that Dori would find love. That everybody did. When I asked her if she had, she said, 'Everybody but me.'" Peg looked pleased. "I'm so glad that's changed."

"She married David Hartford," Alexis said. "He owns Cliffside."

Charlie nodded. "Dori went to a costume party there. She said it's quite a place."

"It's beautiful. Our aunt used to own it and my sisters and I spent a lot of time there as children. Were you shopping for antiques again this morning?" Alexis asked.

Peg made a face. "We wanted to get the kids something for the house that they could all enjoy. It's been three years since they've shared the beach house. We thought we'd leave something special for when we all come back at Thanksgiving."

Something caught Alexis's attention through the coffee bar window and she looked out just in time to see Ferdie leap up, forepaws on Trevyn's chest as the man spoke to him and ruffled his ears.

"Now, there's someone you should meet," Alexis said, waving at him through the window and beckoning him inside. "He's opening a portrait studio in Dancer's Beach. I think a portrait of the two of you for the house would be the perfect thing for your children and their families. Or maybe one of all of you together."

She wasn't deliberately setting out to help him, she told herself by way of excusing her behavior. She just recognized and related to that lost look he'd worn when he'd walked out of the house this morning—as though he recognized his surroundings but didn't feel at home in them. She'd felt that way often enough herself.

He walked into the coffee bar looking fresh and handsome, whatever had been bothering him earlier somehow resolved, at least for now. He brought the perfumed coastal air in with him and Alexis got a whiff of pine, salt and a trace of apples.

Alexis made introductions and related the conversation they'd just shared.

"I told them about you," she said, pushing him into the fourth chair. "But I don't remember all your credentials. Tell them about yourself and I'll get your coffee and refills for the rest of us."

He was clearly startled by her helpfulness and looked just a little off-balance for a moment.

She went to the counter with a smile, delighted to be able to give him a dose of his own medicine.

"I think a portrait of all of us is a great idea," Charlie said as Peg nodded her agreement. "One of our daughters-in-law is a photographer, but she always ends up taking pictures at our get-togethers. It'd be nice if she could be in one without having to set a timer and run back to her spot. What do you think, Peg? Why don't we invite these kids to dinner and talk about it?"

Peg nodded eagerly. "That would be fun."

"We'd like that," Trevyn said, "but there are actually four of us. Her sister is married to my friend and we're watching his two young brothers while they're in the East."

"That's no problem," Peg assured him. "Our family is big on boys so we're used to having them around. I'll fix something they'll like. Was your other sister happy with the egg whip?" Peg wanted to know when Alexis reappeared with a cappuccino for him and the coffeepot to refill Peg's and Charlie's simple cups of coffee.

He remembered that she hadn't asked him what he'd wanted to drink. He must still look as though he needed a double shot of caffeine.

She explained about the accident in the Columbia River and Gusty's subsequent disappearance.

"How awful," Peg sympathized. "I can't imagine anything worse than not knowing what happened to someone in your family. That would make me crazy. We spend most of our time keeping tabs on our children and grandchildren."

"The police are working on it." Alexis swirled the contents of her glass, then downed the last mouthful. "She was spotted at an airport baggage carousel with a man, and it's taken the police weeks to go through passenger manifests and check out everyone."

Peg patted her hand. "That must be so worrisome for you."

"You have to have faith that it'll come out alright," Charlie advised. "Peg gets her nose and her hands into everything, but I mostly just stand back and try to *believe* the situation into coming out for the best."

Peg took offense. "You're suggesting that I meddle?"

Charlie looked surprised. "Are you denying it?"

She thought that over a moment, then smiled from Alexis to Trevyn. "No, I guess not. But there's meddling, and there's creative interference. There's a bit of an art to what I do."

Charlie grinned at their companions. "That's how she excuses being tricky."

"I suppose your mother minds her own business?" Peg asked Trevyn.

"Pretty much," he agreed with a rueful smile. "She passed away when I was in high school. My father retired a year ago, and he's been touring the country on a Harley ever since. I get postcards from everywhere, but I haven't seen him in a while."

Charlie sighed over his coffee. "I've always wanted a Harley."

Peg backhanded him in the arm. "Please. Can you imagine how your arthritis would react to being out in the weather as you travel?"

He gave her a frown. "You don't do it in your Skivvies, you know. You wear leather to protect you and keep you warm."

"Charlie." Peg held her arms out, as though to display her ample form in its navy-blue sweats. "How would this body look on the back of your Harley? Think about it."

Charlie leaned toward her, laughter in his eyes. "Well, I wouldn't bring you, Peggy, my love. I'd find myself a group of road outlaws, then cozy up to some shapely biker babe in leather shorts who can rumble as well as the guys."

Peg stared at him in disbelief for a moment, then burst into laughter. He joined her and they locked fingers on the table as they enjoyed his outrageous scenario.

Alexis turned to Trevyn, who was also laughing. His glance at her invited her to share the moment and she couldn't resist.

The McKeons finally left the coffee bar, setting a date for dinner on Sunday evening.

Charlie gave his wife a gentle shove through the door, then waved at Alexis and Trevyn. "See you Sunday."

Alexis watched them greedily, chin on her hand. "Aren't they every kid's dream of the perfect parents? I mean, I wouldn't want the type that stays thin and looks like an ad for a retirement village, or something. I love that they look so real and comfortable. Like you could take them any problem and even if they couldn't solve it for you, they'd listen and commiserate and hug you until you felt better."

Trevyn pushed away from the table. "Yeah. They're great. I hope their kids appreciate them." He pointed through the window to Ferdie, who now sat at attention, somehow sensing he would soon be freed from his newspaper-stand shackle. "He looks like he could use a cookie."

Athena held up the second half of her biscotti. "Saved this for him." She stood to leave, forgetting the small disposable camera on the table.

Trevyn snatched it up and handed it to her. "Yours?"

"Oh, thanks. Yes. I've been taking photos to paint from. I suppose these are offensive to a professional photographer."

He pushed in his chair. "Not at all. They do a good job for what they are. If you don't want to make adjustments to light or shutter speed or anything, they're good enough. Where are you off to now?"

Alexis felt a hopeful little stir inside her. The time

spent with the McKeons had been warm and cozy, and her enjoyment of them with Trevyn made her feel less alone. He might be part of her family soon. She had to learn to get along with him.

"Nowhere in particular," she replied casually. "I've just been taking pictures."

"My studio's in an interesting old building." He pushed the door open for her. "Want to see it? I rented it before I left for Canada, but now I have to decide how to make it appealing to customers. I've got to be open in a couple of weeks if I'm going to get any of the Christmas trade. Thank you for dropping the McKeons in my lap, by the way."

"Sure." She stepped outside into the cool, overcast day. "You know, Gusty's the one who should see your studio," she said. "She has a gift for decorating. Her home and her classroom are always very inviting."

He gave her a thin smile as she unfastened the dog, who snatched the bite of cookie out of her hand while she worked. "Decorating's not one of your strengths?"

She shook her head as they started down the street, the dog taking the point, tail wagging happily. "I live in a small apartment with a gorgeous view, but spend most of my time at a studio that I share with several other artists. Consequently, except for the occasional milk bottle of fresh flowers, I don't do too much to decorate."

"Isn't it hard to be that far from home? Or is it home now?"

"I'm comfortable there," she replied, "and feel as

though I belong, but home will always be where my sisters are. I get most lonely when I catch cold or get the flu. It makes me revert to childish whining and carrying on. Our mother was never much of a nurse, but Aunt Sadie was.''

''I remember getting some tropical bug on a CIA job in Malaysia. I was sure I was going to die, though all the natives assured me it was nothing. I've never missed home as much as I did then.''

''Does Dancer's Beach feel like home now?'' she asked.

''I love the place. But I can't live on Dave's property forever, especially now that he's married. I've spotted this house in the cove, a sort of bungalow-style with lots of angles and windows. It's on a little knoll surrounded by trees. If it ever comes up for sale, it's mine. Then this will really be home.''

''Any siblings?''

''Just me.'' He stopped in front of an Italianate building on the corner fronted by a series of arches. Within each arch was a storefront. The second one was Trevyn's.

He pulled a key out of his pocket, unlocked the door and reached an arm in to flip on the lights. Then he stepped back to let her in first.

TREVYN LIKED THE SMELL of the place, clean but old, disinfectant mingled with the musty smell of the building that had been here at the turn of the century. A theater in the middle was flanked by three shops on each side.

It was a large, open space with plank-wide strips

of fir making up the wooden floors. The white walls had grown dingy, but two ornate light fixtures, each with half a dozen crenellated tulip shades, hung from the ceiling, obviously left over from the building's earlier employment.

Alexis seemed to like it. She walked into the middle of the room, looked up at the chandeliers and smiled, doing a tight turn under one of them as though imagining herself in a performance.

"The chandeliers lend a lot of charm," she said, then glanced at him with a smile before going to the wall that connected the shop to the next one. "And people who are charmed undoubtedly show it in their faces when they pose."

Now that was an angle that hadn't occurred to him.

She rubbed her fingertips gently over the wall.

"It's ten feet high and thirty feet long. It's going to be a decorating problem, I know. I guess my only recourse will be to hang portraits all over it."

She considered that, then turned and wandered along the other two walls. The front had a large display window, but the other had light switches, a fuse box, a wall telephone and built-in shelves. "Wouldn't they be better in the window? And your counter will have to go here where the phone is. You still have quite a bit of wall space to display portraits and customers can admire your work while they're asking for information."

She looked avid, he thought. As though she were really interested in what he planned to do. But her eyes kept going back to the long blank wall.

"You told me you weren't much of a decorator," he teased, "yet you're thinking like one."

She put the flat of her hand to the wall as though feeling for something. "No, I'm not," she said, giving him a glance over her shoulder. "I'm thinking like a muralist."

A mural. Another angle he hadn't considered.

He went to where she stood and tried to imagine the wall painted with...what?

"You mean like one of those trompe l'oeil things you see in *Architectural Digest?*"

"No." She took a step back and ran her eyes the length of the wall. He guessed she was seeing images. "I'm not sure. Something appropriate to a photo studio. Maybe old scenes of Dancer's Beach. Certainly someone must have some. Or a sort of montage of portraits interspersed with landmarks. Or maybe just the stretch of beach." She took a few steps along the wall and stopped. "The dancers just walking on the beach in white lace and parasols." She smiled, apparently warming to her own idea. "You know, to represent a time when they knew they were safe, maybe already falling in love."

He couldn't quite picture it, but he liked the idea. "And you can do this?" he asked.

She came out of the trance the wall had inspired suddenly and looked at him in surprise. "Me?"

He shifted his weight and folded his arms. "I don't imagine there are too many muralists in Dancer's Beach."

"But we'd be confined in the same space," she

argued, "and you hate me." Then she frowned as though she hadn't intended to say that aloud.

He laughed softly. "Not all the time," he said, knowing an outright denial would not have rung true. They'd had some fairly combative moments since their unfortunate meeting in the dark kitchen. "Or are you afraid you can't coexist with me long enough to get it done?"

"I am," she admitted candidly. "Half the time I want to kill you, and the other half…"

She stopped, apparently thinking better of whatever she'd been about to say. For an instant, he wanted to know what that was more than he wanted anything.

"And the other half?" he asked.

She met his gaze and held it. She made no sound, but he swore he could almost hear the words forming in her mind.

I'm interested in you! her eyes said.

He forced himself not to react to that, though it stunned him to his toes. Because he found her fascinating, more so now that they'd spent some time together without shouting at each other.

But that was no good. Her sister was carrying his baby. And when she wasn't being intriguing, she was damned irritating.

She seemed to regret the momentary slip. "Gusty apparently has feelings for you, so I'll let you live."

"I appreciate that." He straightened his stance and said briskly, "I'll pay you well. By the hour, if you like. I imagine this is the kind of thing that always takes longer than you project."

That did it. Nothing squelched man-woman contact like the mention of money.

She sighed and turned back toward the wall, her eyes narrowed, possibly in calculation.

"I'd need at least…" She named a high hourly rate and a considerable number of hours to finish the mural. She understood that nothing intensified a discussion of money like large figures. "And I can manage to work with you if you promise not to pick at everything I say."

"You just don't like being challenged."

She cast him a dark glance, all "interest" gone from her eyes. "You're already doing it."

He raised both hands in surrender. "All right. I'll watch myself. I'll drive you home and write you a check to get you started."

He expected her to balk at that, but she surprised him with a nod.

Damned woman.

ALEXIS MADE SPAGHETTI and salad for dinner. The boys seemed to find it passable. While they did their homework on the dining room table, she sat curled up in a chair with her sketch pad and prepared several designs to offer Trevyn.

Trevyn. She was immediately distracted from thoughts of planning a mural when she remembered that unsettling moment she'd looked into his eyes in his studio. It was as though something she'd kept under guard so closely even she'd forgotten it suddenly broke free and forced itself to her attention— and his.

God. She'd managed to retain her dignity, but it'd been horrid when she'd looked into his inky black eyes and felt ensnared. Trapped. And it wasn't that she couldn't get free, but that she didn't *want* to.

For that single breath of time, he was the end of her long journey, her safe harbor, the heart of her adventure. She'd felt a connection that was more elemental than anything she'd ever experienced. It had shaken her.

She scribbled viciously through the beginning of a design and turned the page on her sketch pad.

But where had that *come* from? They didn't like each other. And she'd never been a woman who felt the appeal of the bad boy or the dangerous man. She wanted comfort, trust, kindness, affection.

With Trevyn so far all she'd gotten were bruised ribs, harassment, mental anguish and a lot of mouth.

Mouth.

He had a nice one. It was nicely shaped, not thin and not too full. Wide enough for a killer smile.

She rapped her fist on the vacant page. What was happening to her? He belonged to Gusty! Or she, at least, deserved first right of refusal on him once they found her!

Alexis let her head fall back against the chair cushion and closed her eyes in quiet exasperation. For most of her adult life she'd been unable to find a man who appealed to her. Almost thirteen years of rejecting come-ons, or accepting them, then ending the evening early because she regretted it.

And then like a test from heaven on which she

wrote her own large F, she found herself falling for the man who'd impregnated her sister.

Hours later, the boys long ago showered and in bed, she continued the argument with herself.

Actually, it was Bram she should be waiting for. If Athena had been with David the night of the costume party, and Gusty had been with Trevyn, then Bram Bishop, the third Musketeer, had been the one with whom Alexis had spent her time that night.

He'd flirted with her, charmed her, listened to her views on the world and shared his, then danced with her. Unwilling to deceive him further she'd finally run away, certain he wasn't the culprit she and her sisters had suspected.

Trevyn belongs to Gusty, she told herself firmly, trying to make it sink in. Bram could belong to you.

If he ever came home from Mexico.

Chapter Four

Trevyn had a tripod set up with his Hasselblad, a raccoon sighted in the crosshairs of his viewfinder. It caught his scent on a midmorning breeze and straightened, then turned and looked directly into the camera, a chunk of bread Trevyn had planted to lure him caught artfully in his paws.

At the same instant that he clicked the shutter, Ferdie bounded into the shot, barking excitedly. In a blink, the raccoon was gone.

Trevyn straightened and muttered an expletive.

"Ferdie!" Alexis appeared an instant later, the leash in hand. "I'm sorry. Did he ruin a shot for you? I opened the door before I had him hooked up and he got away from me." The apology was offered sincerely, then she frowned with sudden severity. "You don't have to swear at him. He didn't mean to chase your subject. What was it, anyway?"

"A raccoon," he replied, determined not to argue with her. Their quarrels seemed to be generating sparks he didn't need. "And I was swearing at the situation, not at him. Raccoons are plentiful around here." He scratched the dog's ears to prove his claim and was rewarded with a pair of large, damp paws on his chest.

Alexis took advantage of the moment to clip on the leash, then ordered the dog down. She brushed a tiny fleck of dirt off the chest of Trevyn's blue-and-gray-plaid flannel shirt.

Trevyn held himself still but felt the small touch to the core of his bones.

She, mercifully, didn't seem to notice. With the dog leash in one hand, she held up a sheaf of papers with the other. "I had some designs for you to look over, but I didn't realize you were working. Shall we find you later?"

Trevyn capped the lens and slung the camera onto his shoulder. "I'm not really working. I spotted the raccoon while I was walking around and thought I'd immortalize him. But he's got other ideas. Let's see your plans."

She spread the sheaf of papers on a nearby stump and they knelt on opposite sides of it to look them over. She'd given him three choices—a historical view of the building he occupied as it would have looked in its heyday with a couple in appropriate dress looking up at the marquee.

The second design was a sort of composite of Dancer's Beach landmarks with portraits of men, women and children interspersed.

And the third was the one that made her glow when she'd talked about it, a stretch of beach with a curve in the distance showing a few buildings that represented the town. But the focus of the design was the four dancers who'd been headed for the Klondike and whose ship ran aground just off the coast where the Buckley brothers were milling lumber. The relationships formed when the brothers rescued the dancers resulted in the families that founded the town.

This wasn't an image of the rescue, but a speculative glimpse into an outing they might have taken when love was in bloom. The women in Victorian dress and parasols were in the forefront, and the men clustered a distance away, observing, probably congratulating themselves on their good fortune.

There was also something poignant and touching in the uneven numbers—four beautiful women and three tall, handsome men. There was a story there that became the legend of Olivia.

But could he face that image of lost love every working day? Given his own lost Farah? Given the missing Gusty?

She waited for his decision with an impression of patience, but he could feel the tension in her.

Oh, hell. He could live with anything that would bring in the customers and help him get his feet on the ground and eventually help him buy that bungalow on the cove.

He stabbed a finger at the third design. "That one," he said.

"Yes!" She struck out with her free hand and caught him in the shoulder as he moved to get to his feet. He fell back on his backside.

She laughed and reached a hand down to help him up. "Sorry!" Her laughter became an artless giggle. "I got a little overeager there. I'd have thought a trained spy wouldn't be knocked on his duff so easily."

"Yeah," he replied, aware of several levels of meaning there. "So would I. I'm going to town for paint and supplies. You need anything?"

He'd intended to ask her if she wanted to come along, but he was very much aware of her smaller hand holding his, of the sparkle in her eyes and her laughter. And that wasn't good. So he'd altered the question.

"A large roll of butcher paper," she replied. "Then I can work on the layout, tape it on the wall, and we can adjust it."

"Sounds like a plan. Anything else?"

For an instant, their eyes made the same connection they'd made yesterday. But she shook her head, her smile diminishing. "No, that's it. Thanks. Come on, Ferdie. Let's finish your walk."

As though understanding every word, Ferdie headed off at a sedate pace in the direction of the trees.

Trevyn watched them go. Alexis's hair flying out behind her as the wind caught it, the dog raising his nose to sniff the wind and see what he could read in it.

Artistically, they were a beautiful sight.

Practically, they were going to make him nuts.

ALEXIS WAS HAVING LUNCH when Trevyn returned with her roll of butcher paper. He stood on the doorstep, the roll balanced on his shoulder, and frowned at the concoction in her hand.

"What is that?" he asked warily.

"A hot dog," she replied, pleased that she'd thought of it, "wrapped in a tortilla. No hot dog buns in the house."

His expression didn't change. "Dotty usually keeps the pantry and the freezer well stocked."

'Yeah, but I don't cook," she explained. "I mean, I can when I have to—like for the boys—but when it's just me, I don't bother."

"You mean you didn't warm the hot dog?"

She looked at it, then at him. "The package says it's fully cooked."

"Yeah, but it's…" He looked into her eyes, then seemed to decide against an argument. "Never mind. Where do you want this? It's heavy."

She held out both arms, one hand still holding the improvised taco dog. "Right here. I have strong arms. Thanks for picking it up for me."

"Sure." He dropped it gently onto them. "I got a sort of warm beige-yellow color for the other walls. Will that be all right as a base for your mural?"

"Perfect," she replied.

"Good." He hooked a thumb in the direction of the guest house. "I'm going home to make a grilled ham and cheese and a salad. Minimal effort, but some nutrition."

Alexis frowned at his derisive tone. "I'll have you know this had shredded lettuce and chopped tomatoes in it."

He rolled his eyes. "I'll be home all afternoon, if you need anything."

"Thank you, but I won't need anything."

"Or if you lock yourself out." That was issued with a slightly superior smile as he turned away.

She kicked the door closed.

Alexis cut the paper into five-foot segments to make the thirty-foot length more workable. Then she taped together four of the two-feet-high widths to make a tall work area for creating the figures. The top two feet of the wall would be sky.

She moved aside the kitchen table and chairs and spread her work on the flat floor covering. Ferdie watched her interestedly from the other side, apparently sensing that a closer look could get him into trouble.

Alexis petted him for his astuteness and gave him a chewy bone to keep him occupied while she worked.

She sketched out the line of the beach, then created the first female figure, clothing her with turn-of-the-century wear she half-created half—copied from an encyclopedia she found in David's sitting room.

When she looked up again, Brandon and Brady were looking down at her, wide-eyed with surprised respect.

"Wow," Brandon said, squatting down to look more closely. "You're really good."

She'd completed a sketch of the profile on one woman watching another, who pointed to a schooner far out at sea.

Alexis leaned over it, examining every line, then got to her feet with a groan to assess the overall impression. She liked it.

"Yeah, I am, aren't I?" she said with the first creative thrill she'd experienced in a good long time. "One five-foot section done, only five to go."

"What's it for?" Brady asked, squatting down also. "And why is she dressed funny?"

"It's the sketch for a mural in Trevyn's photography studio."

"What's a mural?"

"A painting on a wall instead of a canvas. And they're dressed in the clothes women wore in the late 1800s because murals usually tell a story, and this one is about the four women who were shipwrecked here."

"That's why this place is called Dancer's Beach," Brandon said. "But where are the other women?"

She pointed to the other taped rolls of butcher paper. "The wall is thirty feet long, so I have to do it in small segments. The Buckley brothers who married them and founded the town will be in it, too."

Brady sat back on his heels. "What's for dinner?" he asked practically.

She had that under control. She'd found two cans of chili in the cupboard. "How about chili?"

"Yeah!" Brady was enthusiastic. "Can we have it on a baked potato?"

That, she could handle. "Sure. That okay with you, Brandon?"

"Yeah. With cheese and onions?"

A little grating, a little chopping. She could handle that, too. "You bet. Get your snacks, then TV until five o'clock, okay?"

They leaped over her sketch with heart-stopping but accurate agility.

Brandon talked about school while they ate dinner, and Brady contributed with a little of his old spark.

When David and Athena called shortly after, Alexis got the cordless phone for Brandon while Brady talked on the wall phone in the kitchen.

Alexis cleared the table and filled the dishwasher.

"But it's not a honeymoon," she heard Brady say as she added detergent, then closed the dishwasher door. "It's a business trip. You're going to sell your book and Athena's going to move her office."

Brady's voice seemed to tighten, then she saw his shoulders sag as he said, "Oh. Yeah."

"No, everything's great," Brandon said from his perch on the kitchen counter. "Alexis is a pretty good cook as long as she has cans of stuff to cook with."

Alexis turned to him with a hand on her hip and a playfully disgruntled expression.

Brandon laughed.

They talked for several minutes, then Brady handed Alexis the phone and Brandon turned off the cordless.

"Dave wants to talk to you," Brady said. "I'm going to finish my homework upstairs."

He disappeared in a hurry while Brandon surveyed the contents of the refrigerator. Alexis wandered into the dining room with the phone.

"Is everything all right with Brady?" David asked without preamble. "He sounds...I don't know... testy. Like the morning we left."

She was certain something was wrong, but she didn't want David and Athena to have to worry about it. "The routine's a little different with the two of you gone. I suppose he's feeling a little insecure. Try not to worry. I'm on top of it.''

"Thanks, Lex," he said. "It might help if Trev spends some time with the boys. They know him well and he usually makes them laugh." A wry note came into his voice. "I know you're not wild about him, but if you'd have him over for dinner once in a while, or if that's too hard for you, let the boys go off with him, Brady might lighten up."

Great. "Sure," she said brightly. "I'll talk to him about it."

"Thanks, Lex."

"How're things going? Any serious interest in the book?"

He laughed with a tinge of embarrassment in the sound.

"There is!" Athena's voice answered excitedly. "Three publishers, actually. We're meeting with two of them tomorrow, and the other the day after. We'll let you know what happens."

"You mean I'll be able to say that my brother-in-law is an author?"

"Why not?" he replied. "I'm telling everyone my sister-in-law is a famous artist."

"Liar," she said. "Are you okay, Athena?"

"I'm great. If it wasn't for Gusty being missing, everything in my life would be perfect. Nothing from Holden, yet?"

"Nothing. We call every day."

"Okay. Well, take care of yourself and get Trevyn to look out for Brady, okay?"

She'd heard them the first time. "You bet," she

replied cheerfully. "Sleep tight." She added on a light laugh, "You are getting *some* sleep?"

"*Some*," David replied with the same emphasis. "Talk to you the day after tomorrow. Unless you need us, then call here and they'll get a message to us."

"Got it. Good night, guys."

David and Athena offered a simultaneous good-night, then hung up the phone.

Alexis turned off the cordless and called Trevyn. There was no answer. She looked out the side window and saw no lights on in the guest house. He was apparently out.

Brandon, an open-face peanut butter sandwich on the flat of his hand, walked past her toward the stairs, Ferdie leaping into the air as the boy offered him a bite.

"Still hungry?" she asked unnecessarily.

"Yeah. Maybe I should have two potatoes next time. I'll call you before I go to sleep."

"Okay."

Determined to keep watching for Trevyn, Alexis made a pot of tea and sat at the kitchen table, roughing out ideas for the next section of the mural. And worried about the boys.

She tucked them in just before nine-thirty. Brady was really asleep this time, his breathing soft and even under the thick coverlet.

Brandon had no idea what his problem was. "He's been such a grump," he said with a frown of his own. "I don't get it. I'm not crazy about him anyway, but he's not usually such a pain in the butt."

"Oh, you do too like him," Alexis insisted, bundling his feet. "I have two sisters and I know how annoying they can be, but sometimes they're fun. Especially when you all grow up."

Brandon sighed. "Yeah, well that's going to be a long time. He's only ten."

"You'll survive."

"Maybe."

"I guarantee it. Good night." She patted Ferdie and went back to work on her sketches.

It was after one in the morning and she'd just climbed out of the shower and pulled on a robe when she heard the scream. It was high-pitched and bloodcurdling and felt as though it drove an icy knife right into her stomach. It was one of the boys.

Heart pounding, she ran down the hall to Brady's room and flipped on the light, expecting to find him bleeding or ill at the very least. But the room was empty, his bedcovers half on, half off the bed.

The screaming continued and she followed the sound, confused when she collided with Brandon in the hallway.

"It's coming from David's room," he said, pale and wide-eyed as he pointed to the end of the hall.

Alexis raced him to the room where Brady stood, staring at the well-made bed, still screaming.

She caught his shoulders and turned him to her. His body felt hot and sweaty under the pajama top. His cheeks were bright red, his eyes wide and panicky, though something in them suggested he wasn't entirely awake.

She gave him a small shake as he screamed again,

seemingly oblivious to her presence. "Brady!" she shouted. "Brady! What's wrong?"

"Gone!" he said, pointing to the bed. "He's gone!" He screamed, his voice growing hoarse.

"You mean David?" she asked, shaking him again to reclaim his attention. "Brady! Do you mean David?"

He focused on her suddenly, apparently finally throwing off the last threads of a nightmare. His face crumpled and he fell against her, sobbing.

Panicky herself, she held him to her and sat with him on the edge of the bed.

"Brandon, do you know how to call Trevyn?" she asked quietly as Brady wept.

Brandon was gone like a shot.

TREVYN SAT IN HIS LIVING ROOM, a snifter of brandy in his hand and a copy of David's manuscript on his lap, the pages he'd already read stacked up on the side table.

His friend was more than clever, Trevyn thought. He might even be brilliant. He was only five chapters into the tale of three military friends on a government mission, but the characterization lay the groundwork for solid drama and tight conflict.

Trevyn was grateful that he really couldn't find himself in any of the characters. He'd been afraid when David had told him about the book that he'd see the three of them, their personalities dissected for all the world to see.

But they were very different men from Trevyn and his friends, and though the military situation was familiar, the setting was Kosovo, and the issue was the search for the brutal Serbian president, Slobodan Milosevic.

Trevyn put a page aside and had reached for the next one when the phone rang. He stared at it in surprise for a moment, then glanced at the clock. One-seventeen in the morning.

Worried, he picked up the receiver.

"Trev!" Brandon's voice said anxiously. "Something's wrong with Brady!"

He put the manuscript aside and, without stopping for his jacket, shot out the front door to the main house.

Brandon opened the door as Trevyn ran up the steps.

"They're in Dave's room," he said, pointing to the stairs. "He wouldn't stop screaming!"

Trevyn took the stairs three at a time and followed the sounds of hysterical sobbing to the end of the hall. He stopped in the doorway of Dave and Athena's room to see Alexis in a fuzzy pink robe sitting on the bed and holding a sobbing Brady to her.

"He *is* coming back!" she said forcefully. "He had meetings in New York, remember? He explained it to you."

He saw relief in her eyes when she spotted him. "Oh, Trevyn," she said.

"What happened?" he asked, leaning over them. "Brady?"

The boy's face was tearstained and blotchy as he pushed away from Alexis and reached up for him.

"Dave's gone. I dreamed he was gone. Rocky said he wouldn't come back!"

Trevyn lifted the beefy little boy into his arms and felt his arms and legs wrap around him and cling as though he represented rescue. He sat beside Alexis with him and rubbed his back.

"Who's Rocky?" he asked.

"A kid at school," came the tight reply.

"Does he know Dave?"

"No."

"Then how would *he* know what Dave's going to do? But you know he had to go to New York."

"I know," Brady wept, his body trembling. "But he's not coming back."

Trevyn held him tighter. "Of course he's coming back. He lives here. This is his home. You and Brandon are here."

"Yeah, but we're just..." Brady began, then pressed his lips together and refused to go on.

"Just what?" Trevyn prodded.

Brady shook his head.

"I think he wants to say we're just his *half* brothers," Brandon said for him, moving in to sit on the other side of Trevyn. "He told me that the other day, but I thought he was just being a jerk."

"Hey," Trevyn chided gently.

Brandon looked penitent. "Sorry."

"We're just half!" Brady said with sudden vehemence, leaning back to look into Trevyn's eyes, his own tear-filled and miserable. "Not even whole brothers, just half!"

Trevyn mopped a tear off Brady's face with the

heel of his hand. "And you think that makes you less important to him?"

"I'm just Brandon's half brother and he doesn't like me," Brady said with complete conviction that that was fact. "I'm not a whole kid with anybody," he said, his face crumpling again. "Just Mom and she doesn't care. My dad doesn't want to know me, and I don't even have one whole brother!"

Brady fell against him again and wrapped his arms around his neck.

Trevyn held on, wondering at the tenacity of a child who'd gotten this far with such fears on his shoulders.

"Come on," Brandon said, his voice thick as he gave his brother's back more of a shove than a pat. "I brought you with me, didn't I?"

"But you didn't want to!"

"I had to wake you up, remember? If I didn't want to, I'd have left you sleeping."

Brady considered that but continued to cry.

"And Dave loves us even though we're just half. If he didn't, he wouldn't have custody of us. He wouldn't have let us keep Ferdie. We've been visiting him since we were little. You're just being dopey." At another look from Trevyn, he added more forcefully, "Well, he is. How much proof does he need?"

"Well, you thought we had to *pay* him to take us," Brady reminded him. "That was dopey."

David had told Trevyn about Brandon offering to sign over his trust fund to David if he would let the boys live with him.

"Fear of any kind isn't dopey," Alexis put in.

Trevyn noticed that tears were streaming down her face. "But you should tell somebody when you're worried about things like that. That's what adults are for."

Unfortunately, that hadn't been Brady's experience for much of his life.

She put a hand to the boy's back and rubbed gently. "Something else is worrying you, isn't it? You're still crying."

"Well…" Apparently somewhat buoyed by Brandon's reminder that he'd brought him by choice when he'd run away, Brady quieted a little and swallowed. "It's still gonna be different. Even if he does love us."

"Why?" Trevyn asked.

"'Cause now he's married to Athena."

"I thought you liked Athena," Alexis said.

He nodded. "I do. But Dave said their trip to New York is like a honeymoon."

"And?"

Brady shrugged, then scrubbed away fresh tears. "Honeymoons make babies, right?" He looked into Trevyn's eyes. "Having us was okay when he wasn't married, but now he's gonna have kids."

Trevyn pulled him to him again as he wept anew. He met Alexis's eyes over the boy's shoulder, sure they were finally at the root of his distress. "You don't think a kid takes the place of a brother, do you? I mean, kids are great and everybody should have them, but they keep you up at night when they cry, they're a big responsibility, and you worry about them for the rest of your life." He drew him away again and smiled. "But a brother is a buddy. He helps you out when you're in trouble, when you need a friend, when you need somebody to stick up for you or to cheer you up. Nothing replaces a brother."

Brady blinked and studied him suspiciously.

"It's true," Trevyn insisted. "And when you've got two, it's even better. He and Athena could have ten kids, but he'll always need the two of you."

Brady's brow furrowed. "I dreamed he wasn't coming back. That he forgot us like Rocky's dad forgot him when his other wife had a baby."

"But you know that a dream is just a story going on in your sleep. It isn't real. Dave said they'd be back in a week or ten days. How long has it been?"

"Just three days."

"Right. So he'll be home in eight days, tops."

"Seven!" Brady corrected.

Trevyn grinned. "Just wanted to make sure you were paying attention because this is important. David loves you, and it doesn't matter how many kids he has, he'll always want you with him. Okay?"

"Okay."

"Good. You think you can sleep now?"

"You think you can stay?" Brady asked. "In case I have the dream again?"

Trevyn turned to Alexis and was surprised by her vehement nod. "Please," she said.

"You can have the room next to mine," Brandon said. "This'll be cool!"

Alexis smiled wryly. "Cool," she said under her breath. "You need a glass of milk before you go back to bed?" she asked Brady.

He shook his head and yawned, the emotional event finally taking its physical toll.

"All right, then." Trevyn walked him to his room while Alexis got Brandon settled in. He pulled Brady's blankets up and sat beside him. "You've got this all straight now? Because if you don't believe me, I want to know."

Brady sighed. "I believe you. It's just been so great here, like it's really not supposed to happen to Brandon and me. When Dave went away, I thought maybe that was true after all. Things weren't supposed to be this great."

"Dave didn't go *away* away. He just went on a trip and half of that trip is about making it possible for Athena to move her business back here. So the thought that he wouldn't come back makes no sense at all."

Brady patted Trevyn's arm. "I know." His eyes fluttered closed and he heaved a deep sigh. In a moment, he was asleep.

Trevyn met Alexis in the hallway coming out of Brandon's room.

"Is he all right?" she asked.

"I think so. He's asleep. Brandon?"

"I'm fine," came the reply from Brandon's room. "Do you think they *are* going to have a baby?"

Trevyn leaned into the room. "Probably. Eventually. What do you think about that?"

"I think that'll make me an uncle."

"That's right."

"What'll that make you?"

"Just a friend, like I am now."

A pair of white-patterned pajamas and mussy platinum hair bloomed out of the darkness as Brandon came to wrap his arms around Trevyn. "We'll adopt you, then you could be our brother, too."

Touched, Trevyn hugged him. "Thanks. We'll take care of that first chance we get."

Brandon smiled at Alexis. "We could adopt you, too, but you're already going to be sort of an aunt."

She kissed his forehead. "As long as I'm in somewhere. Good night, Brandon."

AFTER THE BOY WENT BACK TO BED, Alexis beckoned Trevyn to follow her downstairs and into the kitchen.

"You sit down while I get the…" She pointed him to the table, then realized that she'd moved it across the room.

He went toward it and she hurried to help him move it back. "Sorry about that. I was working on my sketches on the floor and needed room."

He frowned at her across the table as they placed it where it belonged. "Look, I know you're not happy about my staying the night, but he was so—"

She stopped him with a raised hand. "That's fine with me. But we do have to talk." She opened the freezer again and dug out a carton of ice cream while he replaced the chairs. "When Dave called tonight, he talked to Brady and thought he sounded upset about something. He thought it would help him if you were around more. I tried to call you tonight, but you were out."

"I went back to the studio and painted two of the walls."

She scooped ice cream into two bowls. "Thanks for coming right over." She didn't know what she'd have done had he not. She'd been able to comfort Brady, but a woman's embrace couldn't provide the same sense of security as a man's strong arms. She'd longed for them often enough throughout her childhood, but her father had spent so much time away. *Away* away.

"You're welcome. Who could ignore a kid in trouble?"

She cast him a dry glance as she replaced the carton of ice cream in the freezer. "You'd be amazed." She carried two bowls of ice cream with spoons to the table and placed one in front of him. "Here you go. Mocha turtle."

He smiled across the table as she sat opposite him. "Free of shell, I presume?"

"Ha-ha. It's coffee ice cream with turtle candies in it."

"I guessed that. I just don't usually eat ice cream at this hour."

She made a gesture in the air with her spoon to sanctify its appropriateness. "It's the best thing. Slides right down if you're upset or too tired to chew."

"Which are you? Tired or upset?"

"Both," she replied, helping herself to half a spoonful. "A few weeks ago I was consumed with worry about myself and my inability to produce art I could be proud of. And now that seems insignificant in view of Gusty being missing and knowing what the boys have been through."

''I know,'' he said. ''Gusty's always in my head, too. I want to believe she's all right and that we're going to bring her home, but the inability to act on that in any way is making me crazy.''

''Me, too. But we have to save our energy for the time when we finally have something to go on.''

''I know. And Brady's going to be fine. I think he listened to his friend and just panicked. He's the one that was always cheerful and hopeful no matter what and probably never dealt with how he really worried about some things. This was probably good for him.''

''I hope so. If you have time, maybe you should do something with them this weekend.''

He nodded. ''I'll think of something.''

After seeing him with Brady upstairs, she was beginning to think that he and Gusty might be happy together after all, and that he'd be a wonderful father to her baby.

They'd have a happy family, she thought wistfully, swirling her spoon in her ice cream. Gusty loved children, and apparently so did he.

''Gusty loves kids,'' she told him, sitting up straighter in her chair, passing him a napkin from the holder in the middle of the table. ''Did you know she teaches third grade?''

He shook his head. ''We didn't do much talking that night.''

Alexis knew this was none of her business, but she couldn't help asking. ''Do you mind telling me what made it possible for the two of you to…to connect so intimately in such a short time? I mean, even in this age of easy sexuality, people seldom make love on a first date, and even less seldom with a perfect stranger on an hour's acquaintance.''

He smiled. It seemed to be directed somewhere else—probably at Gusty and not at her. ''I can't explain,'' he replied. ''She just walked into my space and was everything I needed at that point in time. And, though I know you and your sisters came on to me and David and Bram to get information, once we got past my not knowing anything, she seemed to find me appealing, too. And that's all it takes, you know. Souls touching.''

Souls touching. She had to admire his way with words. That was how she'd felt about her Musketeer—about Bram. But she'd put him out of her mind when she went back to Rome, because she'd been sure she had no potential for maintaining a serious relationship.

Now this man, who belonged to her sister, was making her rethink her attitude in that regard. Not that there was any point in it.

''Yeah,'' she said softly.

They finished their ice cream in silence, then she showed him what she'd done on the mural layout. They knelt on the floor side by side.

''It's a wonderful beginning.'' He appeared serious and sincere as he studied the detail. ''Where will this go?''

''About two-thirds of the way back,'' she said, gesturing with her hands. ''I'll put two other women off to the right here a little bit, then slightly apart from them to give her special focus—Olivia. Then the men kind of huddle on the far right. And there'll be a glimpse of town way in the opposite corner. What do you think?''

''I think you're a genius,'' he replied, still staring at her first section.

She felt inordinately pleased. ''Well, that's a relief. I had visions of it not being what you wanted at all. Artists are very insecure, you know.''

He rolled up the artwork and handed it back to her. ''Aren't we all? So it's all right if I take the room next to Brady's?''

She snapped a rubber band around the paper tube and nodded. ''Yes, of course.''

She swept a hand in the direction of the stairs. ''I'll get you an extra blanket. This drafty old place gets cold.''

After just having admitted to herself that he was the perfect match for Gusty—not to mention the father of Gusty's baby—she was aware of a tightness in the air, and in her chest, as she heard him follow her upstairs and stop beside her in the doorway of the bedroom.

She went to the linen closet, retrieved a blanket and handed it to him.

''You have your own bathroom,'' she said, forcing an even tone of voice, ''and Dave probably has an extra pair of pajamas in his dresser.''

He shook his head. ''Thanks. I sleep in my Skivvies.''

Stupidly, that brought a blush to her cheeks. At least the dim hall light hid it from his notice.

He grinned. ''Since you don't cook, I presume I'm on my own for breakfast.''

"I can make you a Pop-Tart," she teased.

He laughed. "That's better than a hot dog in a tortilla. But isn't using the toaster considered cooking?"

"No. The toaster and the microwave are permitted. And the kettle. Soup cups are some of my favorite meals."

"Lucky for me," he said, taking a step into the room and turning to her with a hand on the door, "that Gusty and not you came to me the night of the party. Otherwise I'd be looking at a lifetime of take-out food."

She experienced a curious, painful twinge. "Yeah," she said. "Lucky. Actually, I can make French toast, but the boys are big on cereal."

"Cereal's fine. I just felt obliged to harass you. Good night, Lex."

"Good night," she replied.

He stepped back and closed the door.

Alexis drew the first even breath she'd taken since they'd started up the stairs. Trevyn was going to be good for her, she decided as she went to her room. Suffering was supposed to inspire great art.

Chapter Five

Trevyn had to find Gusty or this whole situation was going to become so complicated it would require God, himself, to untangle.

Because the first thing he saw when he reached the kitchen in the morning was Alexis's delightfully shapely derriere as she kneeled over her sketches. It was enough to give him a stress-related stroke.

Fortunately, the boys raced past him to catch the bus at that moment, shouting cheerful goodbyes, and he was jolted into maintaining civilized behavior.

She had dressed in her ever-present slim black pants, but today she'd added a pale yellow rib-knit sweater to them. She wore woolly socks and knelt with her ankles crossed. As he watched, she made a long side stroke with her pencil, her upper body following the movement. Her long red hair was bunched at the back of her head in what should have been a messy tangle.

But he thought it looked cute. Cute. He couldn't remember that anything in the past twenty years of his life had occurred to him as cute.

"If you and your sisters are identical," he asked idly, walking into the room, "why is your hair curly and Athena's straight?"

She started at the sound of his voice and sat back on her bottom to look up at him. "Hi," she said. "I go to the beauty shop. Athena doesn't have the time or the inclination."

"Does Gusty?"

Something seemed to slip in her eyes, but she held her smile in place. He felt guilty, but he had to keep reminding himself that there was a missing third party here. And a baby.

"No, she curls it herself," she said, her smile growing fond. "She wears it up a lot, or pulled back. When she played the Southern belle the night of the masquerade, she did her own hair. She's very feminine and…"

He went stock-still, a half smile frozen on his lips. And he was sure the rest of his face reflected the shock he felt. No. It couldn't be. His every instinct said it couldn't be! He squatted down beside her.

"What's the matter?" she demanded, holding the pencil in a tight fist. She looked around herself nervously. "What? What?"

He swallowed. "You said she played a Southern belle."

"Yes."

"At the costume party?"

"Isn't that what we're talking about?" She sounded mildly impatient with him.

He had to appreciate the humor in that. Wait until she knew the rest of it.

"You," he said, unable to believe what was unfolding here, "were the flapper."

"Yes, I had…" She put a hand to her thighs, her fingertips fluttering as though she'd been about to describe the fringe that had hemmed her dress.

Then he saw the point of this strange conversation occur to her. Her eyes widened as she got gracefully to her feet.

"No!" she gasped.

His mind echoed the same thing.

"But," she went on as he straightened up beside her. She pointed the pencil at herself. "I was with Bram! We danced in the conservatory, I asked him about—"

"Why I wanted to live here," he finished for her, getting to his feet. He walked around her toward the other end of the kitchen, remembering all the details of that conversation. "I told you I love it here, that I was starting a new life and I wanted new sights and sounds, new experiences. You said you love chocolate-covered cherries. I told you I love the White Sox."

"Oh, God," she whispered behind him.

"We danced." He turned to face her. "We didn't talk for a long time, we just held each other, then you ran away from me and I chased you and we made love under the tall palm in the corner of the conservatory."

She stared at him for a long moment. "Everything else is almost right, but we did not make love."

"Lexie…"

"I ran." She interrupted his attempt to deride her

for her denial. "You followed, but when I got outside you were no longer behind me. I ran to the car where Athena was waiting."

He couldn't believe what she was saying. "You wept," he reminded her. "I was afraid I'd hurt you or upset you, but you said it was all right, that it was just the first time you'd ever belonged anywhere and that was…" He stopped because the words had shaken him then, as they did now. "And that was in my arms."

NOW SHE WAS COMPLETELY CONFUSED.

She knew he'd been through a lot in the work he and his friends used to do. He'd lost the woman he loved during the mission in Afghanistan and he'd had difficulty adjusting when they came home.

But nothing at all about him, since the moment she met him when he broke into the house last week suggested that he was in any way diminished, mentally or emotionally, by what had happened. If anything, he was the epitome of the intelligent and witty male in his prime.

Yet nothing that he described in such detail had happened.

"Maybe," she suggested, touching his arm, knowing he was upset by her refusal to acknowledge the truth of what he'd said, "maybe you're remembering Farah."

He pulled away from her impatiently. "Lex, give me some credit," he said sharply. "I haven't been that indiscriminate a lover that I can't tell one woman from another."

"But you didn't make love to me!"

Then something apparently occurred to him. He closed his eyes and let his head fall back as he laughed mirthlessly and muttered, "Oh, hell!"

He went to the refrigerator where he knew David hoarded a Zimbabwe blend of coffee and carried it to the counter where he ground the beans, then began to prepare a pot, following each step ritualistically as he tried to grasp what was happening.

She came to stand beside him. "What?" she demanded.

"This," he said, eyes on the pitcher of filtered water that he poured into the holding tank, "has happened before."

"What?"

"The confusion."

She waited for him to explain. When he simply stared moodily at the pot as it began to drip, she shifted her weight. "Well, good, because I've been in a perpetual state of confusion since you broke into this place. What? What are you talking about?"

He straightened, too.

"I think you may be right about this," he said, his tone reluctant. "I get memories confused since... Farah. I had a sort of delayed stress thing going, and sometimes it causes me to recall things in the wrong order, or one memory is superimposed on another that happened at a completely different time and the memories are convincingly real."

"You don't have a memory of making love to me because you didn't."

He gave her a pitying look. "I do have a memory

of it, because for weeks after the party I imagined it happening over and over. But I had no idea who you were. Nobody knew who the flapper had been.''

She looked horrified, astonished, panicky. ''But I remember that night and my Musketeer was sweet and charming and listened to me without judgments or smart remarks and you're...we don't *like* each other.''

''Yeah,'' he said, pulling the pot out before it was filled to pour himself a cup. He took a deep sip, apparently ignoring how hot it was.

''You mean,'' she asked, as though still trying to come to terms with it, ''you were *my* Musketeer?''

He put a hand to his eyes. ''So it seems.'' He realized with the sudden jolt of a rock to the head that the woman he loved wasn't lost somewhere and out of reach. He had to deal with the trauma of having to open his heart to her when years of darkness and Farah's death had seared it closed.

This was immediate. She was here.

And she was calling him *her* Musketeer.

He took another sip of coffee, then dropped the cup to the counter with a bang. ''No,'' he said. ''I'm my own Musketeer. I've always belonged to myself and I always will. That night was a trick of masks and fantasies.'' She was staring at him and he couldn't tell what she was thinking. ''I mean, we've spent enough time together to know that it's clear we were both mistaken, haven't we?''

Yeah. Sure.

Alexis absorbed that vehement rejection with relief. It was one thing for a woman to pine for a man she couldn't have. To admire his virility and his determination from a distance and be forced to accept that it could never be hers.

But when that man was no longer out of reach, when he stood squarely in front of her—free, heart-whole—it would cost too much when he discovered that she really was all bluster and no talent. No cleverness like Athena, no sweetness like Gusty, only Alexis who just didn't fit anywhere.

But, God, it hurt to admit that, to ignore the sunburst of hope she'd felt that instant she'd first realized he'd been hers.

She drew a breath, squared her shoulders and smiled. She knew how to do this. She'd done it hundreds of times. No one ever saw her bleed.

"Of course we have. Whew!" She drew a theatrical hand across her forehead. She went to roll up her sketches and smiled at him easily over her shoulder. "So, let's just forget this whole thing, okay? No more talk about Musketeers or flappers or costume balls. What's the plan for today? Can we take the sketches to the studio and see how they'll look? When we actually see the plan in place—at least, what I've got of it—we might want to make adjustments."

It took him a moment to answer. She kept rolling, fiddling with the rubber band, tightening the inside of the roll with her finger. Anything to avoid turning around.

"The wall's probably dry," he said finally. "But

I was going to move camera equipment down today.
You've got the day off.''

No. She *had* to turn around. She had to *show* him.
''I can help with that. At least until the boys come
home from school.''

''All right. I could use a hand.'' He agreed with
no evidence of reluctance or discomfort, as though
they hadn't just discovered they were the end of each
other's rainbow—only the sun had stopped shining.
''Give me half an hour to load the truck, shower and
change. If you can wait that long, I'll take you to
breakfast.''

She smiled wider. ''Sounds great.''

BY NINE-THIRTY, Alexis and Trevyn had his studio
equipment safely transferred from the truck, to the
back of his studio. They went to Burger's by the Sea
at the other end of Dancer Avenue for breakfast.

''Eggs Benedict,'' Alexis ordered. The middle-
aged waitress with graying blond hair and a Cordon
Bleu apron scribbled on her pad. ''Orange juice, and
milk, as well as coffee, please.''

The woman didn't bat an eye.

Trevyn ordered a bacon and cheese omelette,
handed back his menu, then raised an eyebrow at
Alexis when the waitress walked away. ''Is there
room in those scrawny hips for all that?''

''I'm not scrawny,'' Alexis denied. ''I'm...coltish.
It's my high metabolism. And it isn't nice to point
out a woman's shortcomings—physical or otherwise.
I tend to eat when I'm—''

''Tired or upset,'' he finished for her, stretching

his legs on his side of the booth, confining her to the corner. He frowned into the coffee the waitress had poured. "So you've told me," he added absently.

"You're the one who looks upset." She dunked the tea bag up and down in her cup, strangely disturbed by the grim expression on his face. "Is it anything you can share?"

"It's what I can't share that upsets me." He looked up, a lift of his eyebrows a feeble attempt at philosophy. "I thought I was going to have a family there for a while," he said, his gaze wandering toward the window onto Dancer Street. "Now it seems Gusty isn't mine after all. And the baby is probably Bram's. Or maybe not. I guess we don't know."

"You seemed anxious to be a father," she said quietly, encouraging him to talk. He seemed to want to.

That lift of his eyebrows again, then he took a long sip of coffee. "I was. My father's great, but we've sort of lost touch."

"Because he's motorcycling, you mean?"

"That and my own cowardice, I guess."

His suddenly morose mood made her realize how much she'd come to depend upon his sunny disposition, his positive approach to everything. She had to help him out of it.

"I don't think anyone who's done what you've done can call yourself a coward," she said firmly. "You've risked your life—"

"Death," he interrupted, "isn't the worst thing that can happen to you. Unless it's the death of someone you love."

"Are you talking about yourself now," she asked, "or your father?"

"Both of us." He paused and leaned back as the waitress went by on the run and splashed coffee into his cup. He waited until she was gone before he resumed the conversation. "I could have gone to Northwestern ten miles from home, but I went to U.C.L.A. instead because I couldn't stand to see my father grieving. It took him years to get over losing my mother. Losing her was awful for me, but seeing him looking lost and wounded was even worse. I called all the time, sent him packages in the mail, went home for Christmas but that was it."

"And now you feel guilty about that?"

"I've always felt guilty. But now I know how he felt when Mom died. When Farah died, I finally knew what it meant to have the heart ripped out of you." He shook his head, a gesture he seemed to intend for himself. "And how unspeakable it would have all been if I hadn't had my friends to get me through."

"Is your father angry with you?"

"Not at all. He finally seems to have found himself since his retirement, though. He's having a great time discovering the country."

She leaned across the table toward him. "Trevyn. Why is that bad?"

He inclined his head. "I guess because he doesn't seem to need me at all, and I'd like him to. Or he thinks I don't care."

"If he thought you didn't care, he wouldn't write to you."

"Maybe."

"I'm sorry about Gusty and the baby," she said sincerely. "Maybe Bram—if it is Bram's child— won't want a wife and child and you can tell Gusty how you feel when we find her. Explain that you knew her only in your imagination, but…"

"No," he said, a curious smiling frown on his face. "If it is Bram's baby, that could get me killed."

She sighed. "Possessive?"

"To put it mildly. If the baby's his, he's going to raise it."

The waitress brought their breakfasts.

"You know, we have more in common than we thought," Alexis said, sprinkling her hash browns with Tabasco sauce. "I ran away from my family, too, only my reasons were less noble than yours. It wasn't that I couldn't stand to watch them suffer, but that I didn't want them to see me fail."

He spread apricot jam on his whole-wheat toast. "Fail at what?"

She shrugged as she chewed a mouthful of English muffin and hollandaise-smothered egg. It almost made her forget her troubles. But not quite. "At everything. Athena's always been so competent, and Gusty's always been so gentle and sweet and I…" She rolled her eyes. "I forget half of what I'm supposed to do and I'm usually too frank to be socially acceptable."

"Dave said you got a scholarship to study in Europe."

She nodded. "But I stayed there to work seriously on art instead of coming home because I didn't think anyone could see me fall on my face across an ocean.''

"Good thinking. But you didn't fail, you succeeded. Did your Italian friends celebrate with you like your sisters would have?''

She laughed. "They're warm and wonderful. I share a studio with four other artists and we sustain one another.''

"But you're not interested in any of them?''

She smiled. "Two are women, one is a happily married man and has four little girls. The other claims to adore me, but only when his beautiful and wealthy girlfriend takes off with her alternate boyfriend. And even then he has an eye on a beautiful brunette in the trattoria down the street.'' She reached for the jam.

"Seems your only alternative,'' he said, passing it to her, "is to find a man here and take him back with you. Or move back home again.''

"Or remain single. Single's fine, you know. Lots of women do it and are perfectly happy.''

He was shaking his head before she'd finished.

"Why not?'' she challenged.

He pointed his fork at her. "There's too much in there not to give it to some hardworking stiff who needs you and a bunch of little kids who don't need warm cookies and gourmet meals as much as a warm hug and a bright smile.''

The words hung in the air between them, apparently as much a shock to him as they were to her.

A hardworking stiff and a bunch of little kids were precisely what she wanted. But if he thought that she would make a good wife and mother then why didn't *he* want her?

She knew the instant the same thought occurred to him. Confusion raced across his expression followed by a somewhat aggressive denial.

He tore his eyes from her and glanced at his watch. Then he pointed to her plate. "Hurry up. You're on the clock."

She stared at him for one confused moment, then went back to her breakfast.

They were in the studio by ten-thirty. Trevyn arranged his photographic equipment while Alexis taped her sketch to the wall to see how it related to its space and the rest of the mural as she imagined it.

It looked good.

On her hands and knees on the floor, she laboriously covered the back of the sketch with blue chalk, then taped it up again and retraced the design so that it transferred to the wall. The process was slow and required meticulous attention to detail.

She found an old wooden ladder leaning up against a wall and carried it to the mural so that she could create an ocean beyond the scope of the butcher paper.

"I didn't realize it would be so labor intensive," Trevyn said as he walked through the room, a light on a stand balanced on his shoulder.

"It's a large wall," she replied absently, her mind trying to conjure an image of sunlight on the water that her chalk would follow.

"I didn't realize that you did it by retracing," he

said. ''I thought you just decided what you wanted and did it.''

''I don't have that much confidence in my abilities at the moment.'' She stood on tiptoe on the top rung to fluff out a cloud, stretching to the farthest reach of her arm.

''Whoa!'' Trevyn cautioned. ''Let me get you a taller ladder.''

''This is fine. I've almost...'' She stretched another inch and almost overbalanced with a little gasp of alarm, catching herself on the bucket board as she pitched forward.

Trevyn caught her waist in his hands and swung her to the floor.

''I said, I'll get you a taller ladder,'' he barked at her. ''You want to break your neck?''

Now safe on the floor, she laughed. ''I don't know,'' she teased. ''Am I covered under your insurance?''

His scolding glance told her he didn't appreciate her attempt at humor as he disappeared into the back. He returned in a moment with a taller aluminum ladder. He opened it and placed it for her.

He caught her arm when she stepped onto the first rung.

''You don't lean out on a ladder,'' he said. With her on the step, they were eye to eye. ''If you can't reach, you climb down and move it. This one's light. You can handle it.''

There was a glib answer on the tip of her tongue, but he looked so didactically male as he gave her instructions. And when she looked into his dark-of-night eyes and remembered his insistence this morning that they were all wrong for each other, she didn't know what to say.

In fact, she didn't seem to be able to say anything because she knew he was about to kiss her. And it threw everything inside her into a complete dither.

She'd been courted by an Italian count, a movie producer, several other artists and by a Roman carabiniere. Italian men knew how to make love to a woman.

But as Trevyn studied her features with rapt attention, then claimed her mouth, she had a feeling this would be like nothing she'd ever experienced.

ALL RIGHT, HE KNEW this was stupid. He'd told her just this morning that this—that *they*—wouldn't work. And then he'd made an idiot of himself over breakfast when he'd clearly told her everything he liked about her—without even realizing he liked it. He was an idiot.

Now that he knew Gusty wasn't pregnant with his baby, that he'd spent the night of the costume ball with Alexis, all the restrictions against what he felt for Alexis were lifted.

She denied that she cared, but gave him urgent, desperate looks that had come close to driving him crazy.

Forgetting his earlier denials, he decided to act on what he felt at the moment, and let her put her own construction on it. Maybe she could explain it to him. Her lips were as soft and warm as he'd imagined, and surprisingly without skilled sophistication considering she'd lived abroad since college, and among a group purportedly known for their free living.

She let him take the lead and, though she followed eagerly, she never tried to assume control.

So he maintained it with kisses planted on her face, her throat, the nape of her neck, her wrists, anything not concealed by the yellow sweater.

Then he swore he heard a click inside her, or felt the brightness of a sudden light, or some indicator that something inside her had ignited.

She caught him tightly around the neck and, with her weight leaning off the ladder, he was forced to hold his stance to steady her and, for a delicious period, let her do with him as she pleased.

SHE'D BEEN RIGHT, Alexis thought, as reason shut down under the emotional onslaught of this man's complete attention. Trevyn's kiss was like no other kiss she'd ever had.

The pulse in her throat threatened to suffocate her as his lips moved over it, then blazed a brief trail to the neckline of her sweater.

She'd have ripped off the offending barrier, but he seemed to be enthralled anew by the line from her shoulder to her ear, by her ear itself. A kiss there turned her spine to jelly.

Then his arm came around her to catch her hair and move it out of his way as his lips followed her hairline, then planted kisses on her first few vertebrae.

Italian men, she thought drunkenly, were good lovers primarily because they were so intent on showing you how good they were. But Trevyn's purpose seemed to be to show her how inspiring *she* was.

She claimed his lips the moment he raised his head, fueled by a force inside her she didn't recognize but seemed powerless to fight.

Something burst out of her, feeling fragile at first, then triumphant as Trevyn responded to her with flattering enthusiasm. She felt like a flower springing through cracks in the sidewalk. She'd finally bloomed even though she'd been born in concrete.

The question was, what did she do now?

The answer was, she had no idea. A woman who wasn't really sure what she had to give, couldn't very well give it away, could she? Particularly not to a man who claimed he didn't want her.

She drew her mouth away from Trevyn's, gulping in air. Then she tried to push away from him.

"Don't let go," he warned, a thread of amusement in the words. "There's no longer a ladder under you."

She looked around and realized that when she'd thrown her arms around his neck and put her all into that kiss, she'd also pushed him back several feet from the ladder.

He looked into her eyes and seemed to accept her withdrawal, if a little reluctantly. "Scared yourself?" he asked softly.

"A little," she replied honestly. "Did it scare you?"

For a moment she thought he wouldn't answer, then he seemed to make a difficult decision, judging by the furrow on his brow. "It isn't fear," he admitted. "But now that I know I'm not about to be a father, I don't want to go that deep."

He lowered her so that her feet touched the floor. "What stopped you?"

Though it hurt and further confused her, she couldn't fault him for his candor. She hoped he'd appreciate her own. "Lack of experience, I guess."

"Physical experience?" It was a gentle question.

"No. Though I don't have a lot." She hitched a shoulder shyly. "Some. But I meant emotional experience. Experience in giving."

"Giving scares you?"

She shrugged. "I've never done it selflessly. My mother didn't love us. She kind of liked Athena because she fought her, but she thought I was a dreamer and Gusty a coward."

"Athena loves you," he said. "She wouldn't if you hadn't been able to give her something emotional that she needed."

Alexis sighed. "I don't know. When we were children, all I could think about was that my mother might love *me* at least, if my sisters were out of the way. I used to imagine her and I together as though they'd never been."

"Well, what sibling hasn't wished the others had never been born? That only means you're normal."

"I don't think so. I've managed to turn off every relationship I've had." She gave him a small smile. "I turned you off."

"But we didn't have a relationship. You attacked me with a frying pan and I pinned you to the floor."

"As a mating ritual, it lacks something." What

was going on here? "Are you saying we should have one?"

"A mating ritual?"

"A relationship."

He gave the ladder a shake to make sure it was steady, and reached to the floor to pick up the chalk she'd dropped. "I don't think so. Do you?"

"I don't know. You're not being very clear. Maybe it was…just a kiss?"

"When it stops your brain activity," he said, "and you can't find your pulse, it's not just a kiss." He kissed her knuckles, then dropped her hand. "Get to work. It's almost time to break for lunch."

Alexis doubted her ability to get through the day after that, but Trevyn was his nonromantic, cheerfully combative self again and the subject of their kiss was not mentioned the rest of the afternoon.

Chapter Six

"What was your mother like?" Alexis asked Trevyn as they drove home. The boys would be home soon and she had to think about dinner.

He smiled pensively at the road. "All the things a mother should be. Gentle, warm, tough. She was sick for a year, but she kept our lives as normal as possible until she just couldn't stand any more. Then we had a hospital bed in the living room and she issued orders and gave hugs from there."

Alexis felt her eyes and her throat fill, certain Trevyn's mother had been more of a parent from a hospital bed than hers had ever been in perfect health.

"I came home from a football game one night and the ambulance was there." He hesitated, shifted a little in his seat as though the memory still hurt, then finished quietly, "My dad was sobbing. She was gone."

"I'm sorry." Her voice was barely there, too. "But it sounds as though you were very lucky."

"I was."

"Where's your father now? Certainly the weather's

going to get too tough for motorcycle travel pretty soon.''

"I got a postcard from Charleston about a month ago.'' He turned up the driveway to Cliffside. ''He was headed south. I imagine he'll winter in Florida like all the other snowbirds.''

"You should invite him to visit here,'' she said with sudden inspiration. ''There's lots of room. Even if he couldn't come until Athena and David are back, he could have my room, or we could double up the boys or something.''

Trevyn had thought about that before. But what if his father rejected the invitation? Made some excuse why he couldn't come?

She seemed to read his mind. ''If he says no, you'll know you've made the effort. Rejection never killed anyone.''

In view of what she'd told him about the trauma her mother's rejection caused Alexis and her sisters, he wondered at the advice.

"I know,'' she admitted with a sheepish grin. ''Easier said than done, especially by the one giving the advice. But it's worth a shot, isn't it? If you're serious about having a family, your children will need a grandfather.''

That was a little cart-before-the-horse, but ultimately, she was right.

"Can you write him General Delivery?''

He nodded. ''He said he was going to visit friends in Jacksonville, maybe stay a couple of weeks. I can call them.''

"Perfect.''

He opened the garage with the remote and pulled into the dark interior.

"You want to join us for dinner?" she asked abruptly. "I bought one of those all-in-a-bag meals with everything included. You put it in a frying pan for fifteen minutes." She grinned. "Even I can't screw it up. Six o'clock?"

He hesitated. He'd been honest with her. He didn't want to go as deeply as knowing her was threatening to take him. Gusty and the baby had been one thing; he'd been willing to take responsibility for the situation.

But getting to know a woman who would also get to know him without the binding element of a baby between them would never work. He was pretty ugly inside.

"Oh, for heaven's sake," she said impatiently. "I do not have designs on your virtue. *You* kissed *me,* remember, and though we both enjoyed it, we're both smart enough to know there's nothing there. At least nothing binding." She leaped from the truck, yanked her big purse out after her and slammed the door.

He jumped down and met her outside the garage.

"I only asked," she went on, "because David wanted you to spend more time with the boys. But if it's too…"

She turned around to start toward the house.

"I'll come," he said. "You want me to bring anything?"

"No."

He watched her graceful but offended stomp toward the door and had to ask. "Got your key?"

"Ha-ha!" she replied without turning around.

THE CHICKEN, PASTA AND vegetable dish was really very good. Alexis tasted it with great relief, saw the boys look at each other, then at Trevyn with pleased surprise.

"It's good, Lex," Brandon said. "Almost as good as Dotty's cooking."

"Thank you." She considered that a high compliment in view of the housekeeper's extensive, varied and very delicious culinary repertoire.

"You guys want to come with me tomorrow to the vintage car show in the valley?" Trevyn asked. "It's an all-day thing. We'll leave early, we'll—"

"Yeah!" The boys replied simultaneously before he'd even finished.

"How fast do they go?" Brady asked eagerly.

"Not fast," Trevyn replied. "They're just on display, but there's some pretty cool stuff. Some of them are seventy and eighty years old."

"Oh." Brady sounded disappointed. "*Old* cars. No races, or nothing?"

"No. Just beautiful old vehicles with all this great old stuff new cars don't have anymore. There's lots to eat and booths with cool things to buy."

"All *right!*" Brady's enthusiasm reignited at the mention of food and the opportunity to spend money. He turned to Brandon. "Can you lend me some money?"

"David left your allowance for a couple of weeks," Alexis said. "Don't worry about money."

"Can you guys be ready by seven?" Trevyn asked Alexis.

"I have things to do," she replied quickly. "But the boys will be ready."

"Why can't you come?" Brandon asked.

"I'm painting a mural on the wall, remember? I've got to get some extra time in if he's going to be able to open his studio by the middle of the month. I'm not much for cars, anyway."

"But there's food and stuff to buy!" Brady reminded.

Trevyn pulled his key ring out of his pocket, removed one of the keys and handed it to her. He smiled teasingly as she took it. "It's my only one, so don't forget it, or leave it in the studio when you come home."

She made a face at him. "One time I forget my key and you provide a lifetime of key jokes?"

"Just a friendly reminder."

"Nice of you."

She served ice cream and store-bought cookies for dessert and the boys declared dinner a complete success.

They helped Alexis clean up.

"There's a baseball game on TV tonight," Brandon said. "Chicago and New York for the American League pennant. Can we watch it since there's no school tomorrow?"

"As long as you're willing to do your homework Sunday afternoon."

"Yeah."

"All right." Despite his assurance, Alexis knew

she should brace for a battle Sunday afternoon anyway.

Brady saw Trevyn glance at his watch and caught his arm. "You're not going back to the guest house, are you?"

Trevyn ruffled the boy's hair. "I am. You're not worried about Dave anymore, are you?"

Brady caught his arm and held on to it with both of his. "No, but we made you a brother so you should stay *here*." He looked to Alexis for support. "And she's like our aunt, so it's okay."

Trevyn opened his mouth, presumably to offer an excuse why he shouldn't stay.

Alexis, feeling perverse and pleasantly obstructive, said cheerfully, "Of course he can stay."

Trevyn sent her a threatening look.

"If you're leaving early in the morning you may as well be here anyway," she said, ignoring his expression.

His attempt to reply was thwarted again, this time by the ringing of the telephone.

Brady picked it up. It was David.

The boy told him in vivid detail about a boy at school who'd dislocated his arm on the monkey bars. "His arm was stickin' out really weird and Lucy Biederman threw up all over Mrs. Cutter! It was so cool. And guess what? Trev's living here now."

Trevyn went to Brady and made a beckoning gesture for the phone.

"Hold on, Dave," Brady said. "Trev wants to talk to you."

Alexis left the room as Brandon moved closer, waiting for his turn on the phone.

She didn't want to examine just why she'd come out on Brady's side. She just knew there was a certain satisfaction in seeing Trevyn discomfited, particularly when he could so easily tell her he didn't want "to go that deep."

She picked up the boys' jackets off the sofa and hung them up in the closet. She shook out the table-cloth, replaced the pot of flowers that always sat in the middle, pushed the chairs back in.

She should check the boys' clothes, she thought, to make sure they had something presentable to wear to dinner at the McKeons' tomorrow night.

My, wasn't she getting domestic? She expected to want to laugh at herself and was surprised to find that she didn't. She'd never imagined she had such qual-ities and it was a little startling to find that they lurked under the carelessly free and disconnected attitude of the artist that owned her soul.

What did that mean?

"Lex?" She snapped out of her thoughts to see Brandon standing in the doorway. "Athena wants to talk to you."

She went to take the phone.

"Lexie! Thank you!" Athena sounded more than pleased with her. 'I know it isn't easy for you to coexist with Trevyn, but David's so relieved that he'll be there all the time. Brady sounds two hundred per-cent better already. How's the cooking going?"

"Did the boys complain?" Alexis asked worriedly.

"No. In fact, quite the opposite." Athena laughed

lightly. "I was wondering if you'd brought in a caterer."

Alexis had to laugh with her. "No, I've just discovered every pre-prepared meal in the freezer at the market. Mercifully, Dotty will be home on Monday."

"Well, I appreciate your efforts. I know you didn't go to Cliffside expecting to end up with the care and feeding of two young boys."

"No, I didn't. But all our lives seem suddenly to be full of surprises. Besides, it's been very educational."

"Really?" Athena sounded suddenly alert. "In what way?"

"Just interesting." Trevyn and the boys had wandered off, presumably to watch the ball game. "Tell David I wish him luck with the third publisher."

"I will. Take care of everyone, Lex."

"Right."

She hung up the phone, considering herself lucky that, though she'd longed her whole life for love and security, she'd never needed anyone to take care of *her*.

TREVYN FOUND COMFORT in the beautifully kept and beautifully restored machinery. And in the boys' fascination with the old cars, despite Brady's disappointment that they didn't race.

He wished Alexis was here, even though he relished a day away from her and the turbulence she'd brought about in his life. She would have appreciated the charming old boxy design of the family cars, the streamlined quality of the luxury vehicles fitted with picnic baskets and golf bags, the no-nonsense look of the post-war cars designed for young families with a sensible eye on the future.

"Wouldn't it be cool if *you* had one of these?" Brady asked. He swept his hand to encompass the broad meadow covered with beautifully painted and chrome-polished classic cars.

Brandon pointed to a green and black Duesenberg standing out from the rest like fine art. "I think you should have that one, Trev."

Trevyn was drawn to it like a hungry child to gooey chocolate. He couldn't help himself. It had elegance and style and somehow reminded him of Alexis.

Even as he acknowledged that it was a crazy thought, he understood why his mind made the connection. It was part delicious art and part impeccable engineering—a fanciful, sensitive brain in a perfectly formed body.

All right, that was nuts even for him. And he was sure she wouldn't appreciate the comparison.

"This would look great," Brandon said, "in the driveway of that house on the cove that you showed us when we left Dancer's Beach this morning."

"It would," Trevyn agreed. "Except that it's probably not for sale. Most of the cars here are part of somebody's collection."

"Not so." A woman he guessed to be in her middle-to-late seventies suddenly appeared beside him in a dark flowered dress, the tail of a long scarf around her neck picking up the early afternoon breeze. "I'm here to unload the Duesie,'' she said with a wide smile.

She had short white hair cut closely around her face except for a spit curl on each side in the flapper style.

Flapper style. He thought of Alexis again.

''My husband and I went on our honeymoon in it,'' she said, going closer and running a hand lovingly over the top of the door.

Brady went to touch the gleaming fender, but Trevyn caught his hand and pulled it back.

''Vermont,'' she went on. ''It was October. The sun was golden and the leaves were turning, and the air smelled like a wild garden.'' She closed her eyes and drew in a breath, and Trevyn knew she was reliving the past. ''Henry was an adventurer. He had big ideas and absolutely no fear. He started a leather goods factory in Manhattan with a thousand dollars he borrowed from the bank, and his cousin as bookkeeper.''

She was quiet for a moment, but her eyes were still closed, her lips still smiling.

Trevyn would have respected her private moment, but Brandon apparently couldn't stand it. ''What happened?'' he asked.

''We all worked day and night,'' she replied, spare gray eyelashes fluttering. ''We peddled samples around, got a few orders, filled them quickly, got more and more…'' She opened her eyes again, back among them. She smiled at Brandon and put a hand to his blond hair.

He stood stock-still, aware that she was something special.

"Ever heard of Lassiter Leathers?" she asked.

Brandon shook his head. "No, ma'am."

"I have," Trevyn replied, amazed. "My father gave me a Lassiter briefcase when I graduated from college. It's traveled all over the world with me and it's still in perfect condition. And didn't I read that you upholstered the Royal Family's limos?"

She nodded, putting her free arm around Brady. "I'll bet you've never heard of us, either," she teased.

Brady shook his head. "But I never know what's going on."

She laughed. "Henry made a bundle, we raised two handsome boys that looked a lot like the two of you when they were growing up."

There was tragedy coming in the story. Trevyn saw it in her eyes before she sighed and gave the boys a squeeze. "Lost them both in Korea. Henry died of a broken heart, I think."

The boys looked stricken.

"I'm sorry," Trevyn said.

She shrugged philosophically. "If you're afraid of being hurt, you can't play the game. I had everything—but no one gets to keep it forever. So…" She dropped her arms from the boys and came to stand beside Trevyn like a very elegant used car salesman. "You interested in my Duesie?" she asked.

The boys gasped.

"It's a beautiful car," he said, trying hard to resist everyone's enthusiasm, "but I'm involved in a career

change right now and just starting a small business.''
He smiled in self-deprecation. ''And I don't think it's
destined to rival Lassiter Leathers. I'm afraid I can't
afford it.''

''But we haven't even talked terms yet.''

''Thank you, but whatever they are, I can't afford
them.''

''Easy down?'' she said. ''Small monthly payments for as long as it takes?''

Temptation stood on his shoulder, breathed down
his neck.

She offered her hand. ''My name's Clarissa, by the
way.''

It felt bony and fragile in Trevyn's. ''Trevyn
McGinty,'' he said. ''My friends, Brandon Bjork and
Brady Caldero.''

''The photographer?'' she asked.

Astonished that she knew his name, Trevyn nodded.

''I spend a couple of months every spring with my
sister in Chicago. I remember your photos of a group
of teenagers at a drug rehab center. You could see
the past in their eyes and a very present pain. Your
work is powerful. You probably did more to renew
their funding than all the political speeches made on
their behalf.''

''Thank you,'' he said, humbled by her praise.
''The reporter on the story was very good.'' He remembered clearly David's emotion as they'd talked
to the young people, and his impassioned column that
had followed.

''That settles it,'' she said with sudden firmness.

She went to the car where her purse sat in the driver's seat and extracted a business card. She tucked it into the pocket of Trevyn's blue woolen shirt. "I'm saving it for you. When you can send me your down payment, I'll drive it out to you. I'm in Eugene for the month of October."

"Clarissa, I…" he began to protest, but she patted his pocket.

"I'll be waiting. I want to know the car's going to someone who'll love it." She smiled again. "Life journeys are all about packaging, you know. If you know you're in something wonderful, the ruts and the bumps don't jolt you half as much. If at all possible, I'd like to see you take your journey in my Duesenberg."

Trevyn stared at her, feeling as though he'd just been wrestled to the ground by Goliath in a silk scarf.

He offered his hand. "I'll be in touch, Clarissa."

She took it. "I'll wait for your call, Trevyn."

"What's Careera?" Brady asked as they waited in line for corn dogs.

"Korea," Trevyn corrected. He explained simply, if a little inaccurately, "It was a war where a lot of American soldiers died."

"It's too bad her husband had to die, too," Brandon said. "Are you gonna buy the car?"

"I don't think so."

"Would the bank let me lend you the money from my trust fund?"

Trevyn looked down at him, surprised and touched. It was amazing that a boy from whom so much was taken could still be so generous.

"I appreciate that offer, Brandon," he said, "but I don't think you can do that. And I wouldn't want to anyway. That money's yours. Someday you're going to have big plans for it."

"Maybe Dave can lend it to you if he gets lots of money for his book."

Trevyn laughed softly. "And that'll be *his* money. But it's nice to know you're looking out for me. If I'm destined to have it, I'll find a way."

"Destined?" Brady asked.

How did he explain destiny? Trevyn wondered.

"Sometimes," he began hesitantly, "if you're supposed to have something, or something's supposed to happen to you, it doesn't matter where you go or what you do, what's supposed to happen has a way of ending up in your path. That's destiny—what's *destined* to happen to you."

"Oh."

They'd reached the head of the line and Trevyn placed their order. The middle-aged man in a baseball cap behind the counter handed Brandon a paper plate covered with a corn dog, curly fries and a small plastic cup of coleslaw.

He filled a plate for Brady, but when he reached for the corn dog, two had apparently fused together either in the freezer or the deep fryer and couldn't be pulled apart.

He handed it to the boy with a wide smile. "Looks like you got a double whammy there, son," he said.

Brady looked at his plate with wide-eyed delight. "Sometimes destiny," he said to Trevyn, "is great stuff!"

Chapter Seven

Alexis worked on Trevyn's mural for hours. She'd brought Ferdie and his blanket, snacks, bottled water, a can of pop, and a portable CD player David had told her she was welcome to use.

Ferdie curled up happily on his blanket while Alexis worked to the strains of Billy Joel. She might have preferred something more classical, but found that his "River of Dreams" had something in common with her broad expanse of ocean in the middle of the mural, and seemed to lend inspiration to its creation.

She and Ferdie took a walk after lunch, then one in the middle of the afternoon. They came back to the studio and shared a doughnut from the bakery at Coast Groceries. Alexis stretched out on the floor for half an hour and Ferdie lay companionably beside her, resting his head on her stomach.

The mural was going well, Alexis thought, seeing the completed image behind her eyes. A little thrill of creative excitement shot through her. It wasn't the fine art she'd tried so hard to pull out of herself since she'd moved to Rome, but it spoke to her—the defining quality of all art, fine or commercial.

It was strange that such a stressful situation—her sister missing, the sudden placement in her care of two young boys, the proximity of a man who kissed her like a lover one moment but claimed not to want to be attracted to her the next—should be conducive to something as elusive as creativity.

She'd had perfect conditions in her studio in Rome, yet the spark had escaped her for months. And now she was beleaguered on all fronts and it held out its hand.

Well, she wasn't going to worry, she was just going to go for it. And the moment they found Gusty, she was out of here and back to Rome to be the artist she'd always wanted to be.

The lonely but producing artist.

She got up and worked another few hours. Trevyn had told her that he'd take the boys to dinner, that she shouldn't worry about it. But it was getting too dark to work even with the lights on. She cleaned off her brushes and stood back to admire her work.

There were four dancers now, Olivia slightly apart from them, their skirts billowing in the coastal breeze, a boat visible on the ocean that had taken shape today. She'd done well. A few more days and she'd have the Buckley brothers in, then it would be a matter of detailing, glazing, and the mural would be ready for Trevyn's clients.

She took Ferdie home and was surprised to find the light blinking on the answering machine. She pushed the button, expecting to find a message from Trevyn that he and the boys would be later still.

But it was a message from Officer Holden in Astoria.

"Just wanted to let you know," he said, "that we've finally reviewed all the passenger lists that went through that particular carousel that day, and we have three couples we'll have to investigate further. They might or might not tell us anything, but I'll be in touch either way."

Alexis called him right back, but he'd left for the day. Another officer read her his report, which included the same information he'd left her on the answering machine. She called Athena and David in New York and played the message over the phone.

"Thank God there's *something*," Athena said. "Maybe I should come home."

"Don't be ridiculous," Alexis scolded her. "Do what you went to New York to do, and if they uncover anything that requires you to be here, I promise I'll call you right away. And, Athena? There's something else."

"What?" Athena asked warily.

"Trevyn isn't the father of Gusty's baby," Alexis reported. "He was with me that night."

"But he remembered making love to her!"

"A complication of his emotional distress after their last job. His memories get entangled and confused, or something."

"Oh…Lex." Athena hesitated a moment. "Are you upset? Is he?"

Upset? Interesting word. "We're both a little surprised. But we're doing fine."

"Hold on." Athena's voice faded as she explained briefly to David what had happened.

"He says don't hurt each other before we get home. Think of the boys." Athena's voice had an edge of humor. "You promise you'll call if you need me?" she demanded. "For any reason?"

"Promise. What's new on the book front?" Alexis was eager to move on to another topic.

"We just got back," Athena said. "And it seems we have a deal."

"You're kidding!"

"No. Here. I'll let David tell you."

"Hi, Alexis." His voice was cheerful. "I'm so happy to hear that we might finally have a clue. Are you sure you don't need us to come home?"

"Positive," she replied. "I'll let you know what's happening after I talk to Holden in the morning. But what's this about your book?"

He explained modestly that he'd been given a six-figure advance for a two-book contract. "I can't imagine I'll be a literary star," he said, "but Baldwin Books seems to think so. How're the boys?"

She told him about their trip to the valley to take in the vintage car show. "Brady wasn't thrilled that they don't race, but he sounded happy about going."

"Thanks, Lex," he said, his voice sobering. "I know having Trev around isn't easy for you."

That was certainly true, she thought, though probably not precisely in the way he imagined.

"I'm grateful that you're in agreement with him staying at the house."

"It's not a problem. Oh, and we're all going out to dinner tomorrow night at the McKeons. Apparently Athena met them when she first arrived, they saw me in the coffee shop and mistook me for her. We got to talking and it turns out they need a family portrait taken, so we've been invited to dinner to talk about it. You might want to call early, or wait until the following day."

"We're off to D.C. tomorrow night anyway," he said. "But we'll call you Monday evening from there. Unless you get information about Gusty, in which case we're staying at Athena's place. Leave a message there and we'll get right back to you."

"Got it."

He put Athena back on the phone, Alexis assured her one more time that she'd call if there was a significant development about Gusty, then she hung up.

Shortly after eight o'clock, the boys burst in, followed by Trevyn. Ferdie leaped all over them excitedly.

They told Lexis an almost indecipherable tale about a green car, a beautiful old lady, a double corn dog and a surprise.

She tried to sort things out one by one. "What kind of a green car?"

"A Duesenberg," Brandon said. "Only she called it a Duesie."

"Who?"

"The beautiful old lady," Brady replied. "Me and Brandon look like her sons who died in Careera."

Trevyn poured three glasses of milk. He held up the carton to Alexis. "You, too?"

She held up her cup of coffee and shook her head.

"Henry died of a broken heart," Brandon said as he carried a bag of cookies to the table. "He was their dad. And the one Clarissa had the honeymoon with in the green car."

"Clarissa?"

"The beautiful old lady." Brady frowned at her. "Aren't you listening? Trev's gonna buy her Duesie 'cause life's journeys should be in something really cool, then you don't notice when you fall into a hole."

That didn't entirely come together but Alexis focused on Trevyn. "You're going to buy a classic Duesenberg?"

He shook his head. "Can't afford it." He tapped the pocket of his shirt. "She insisted I take her card, but I can't in all good conscience buy it when my studio won't break even for a year or more."

"She said you could make a low down payment, and low monthly payments," Brandon reminded him. "I think you should do it." He smiled. "Otherwise you'll feel all the ruts and bumps." His smile widened. "Me and Brady must be on our journey in an old truck with no shocks. Like yours."

"Hey!" Trevyn pretended to be affronted.

The boys laughed and went to watch television.

When they were out of earshot, Alexis told Trevyn about Officer Holden's message and her call to the station. "They said he'd be there in the morning."

His eyes widened. "I don't believe it. A clue at last? Maybe?"

"I hope so." Out of nowhere, unbidden, tears filled Alexis's eyes and spilled over.

Trevyn came to her and knelt beside her chair. "Hey. You don't cry over *good* news."

She'd showered and brushed her hair just before he and the boys had come home, and he pushed the unruly red mass back now to touch her cheek. "Unless, of course, you never cried over the bad news, then maybe you're entitled."

She put a hand over her eyes. "If I cried," she said, her voice strained, "it would mean she was hurt or...dead. But if I sucked it up, she could still be fine. Lost and all alone, but fine."

She heard him get to his feet, then felt him catch her elbows and pull her up. He wrapped his arms around her and held her close.

"She is fine," he told her firmly. "If she belongs to Bram, then the cosmos knows better than to let anything happen to her or there'll be hell to pay."

"Then where is he?" she demanded tearfully. "Why doesn't he come home and find her?"

"He probably doesn't even know she's missing," he told her gently. "Or pregnant, or he'd have been here."

She sighed against him, and firmed her grip. "She's always been the gentle one, the one who'd do anything for anybody. What if they don't get along? What if he doesn't *want* a baby? What if he doesn't want her?"

"He's tough and it isn't wise to cross him, but he's

one of the most honorable men I know. Let's wait until we find her and he comes home before we decide it isn't going to work between them.''

She sighed wearily. ''When this is over,'' she said, leaning back to put her hands comfortably on his chest, ''I think we deserve a month on a sun-drenched beach somewhere.''

He raised an interested eyebrow. ''Together?''

She shrugged. ''Why not? Now that we've established that neither one of us wants big things from each other, we can just be comfortable together. We'll go to the Mediterranean and I'll show you all the art galleries. There'll be great stuff for you to photograph.''

''Sounds good to me,'' he said.

HE WAS ABOUT TO LET HER GO—happy that she'd stopped crying, happy that she hadn't mistaken his offer of comfort for anything more—but his fingers clasped behind her waist didn't seem to respond to his brain's command.

Her eyes were the same color as Lake Michigan in the summer and appeared as deep. She'd pulled herself together, but he could still see her fear for Gusty under the surface control.

Her pink cheeks were tearstained but had a satiny quality under the light. They were upturned toward him as she waited expectantly for him to free her.

He put a hand to her left cheek, brushing her wild hair away and tracing the contour with his fingertips.

Her lips parted. They were free of lipstick after her long day at work, and invitingly soft and full.

Even as his brain told him he shouldn't complicate something they'd worked out so comfortably, he felt the slight pressure of her stomach against his groin and suddenly comfort in a complicated situation didn't seem to matter a damn.

A conflagration swept through him from his toes to the top of his head, centering where their bodies touched, heating despite the barrier of clothing.

As he combed a hand into her hair and lowered his mouth to hers he remembered absently that he'd told her he didn't want to go this deep. And as she ignited in response to him, her body sliding against his as she stood on tiptoe to wrap both arms around him, as her mouth welcomed his, moved with it, opened for it, he felt the ground fall away. He had the sensation of spiraling down, down in the silken confines of her embrace.

The only other time he remembered really losing control was when Farah died. But this had nothing to do with death, and that was what made it most alarming. This was all about life, about hearts thundering, pulses ticking, blood racing. His nerve endings quivered with sensation. His entire body was suddenly one tall sensor.

It was as though he'd awakened from a long, long sleep.

ALEXIS FELT HER HEART GROW too big for her chest. It seemed to be the receptor for every feeling Trevyn's hands created as they swept down her spine, shaped her hip, held there a moment pressing her to him, then stroked upward again. Sensation followed his fingertips until her entire torso felt too alive for the rest of her body.

She was going to burst.

He kissed her until she couldn't breathe. And she realized that if the boys weren't on the other side of the house, she'd rip away the clothing that separated them and wrap herself around him right there.

This was art—brilliant strokes, passion, heart and soul engaged in the creation. She could give herself to this.

But her sister was missing. That fact lay at the heart of every thought she formed. She couldn't fall in love with Gusty missing.

She wedged a space between herself and Trevyn and gasped for air. He leaned his forehead against her chin, breathing deeply himself—and suddenly the realization that he could do that when he had a good eight inches on her made her push away a little farther to assess their positions.

Only there weren't two positions. There was only one.

"Wha—?" she began to ask.

His eyes still languid with desire, he managed to grin at her. "You appear to be climbing me," he said, tightening his grip on her. "I like the way you get into a kiss."

She did indeed have one leg wrapped around him, the sole of the other foot braced against his knee.

She groaned and dropped both feet from him. "It was art," she said. But she no longer understood her art, couldn't reach it...couldn't *do* it. And art had always been her life. She felt as though there was nothing left of her. At least nothing to *give*. "I was involved. Will you let me go?"

He did and she tugged down her paint-spattered shirt and tugged up the waistband of her equally disreputable jeans.

He rested a hip on the edge of the kitchen table and ran a hand over his face, clearly as shaken as she was.

"You have to stop kissing me," she said a little stiffly, taking her coffee cup from the table and drinking deeply.

It was cold and she grimaced, taking it to the sink and dumping it. She looked toward the coffeepot, but it was empty.

Brandy. Maybe brandy would help.

"Then you have to stop looking like that," he countered, taking the coffeepot to the sink and rinsing it out, discarding the used filter.

She pulled down the can of coffee. "Like what?"

"Like you want me to kiss you."

"I don't!"

He glanced at her as he put coffee in the filter. His eyes told her it was futile to deny it.

"All right, I do want you to kiss me," she admitted, folding her arms and standing beside him as he finished the process and turned on the coffeepot. "But it comes upon me without warning. One minute I'm fine with you being just a friend and then..." she waved a hand helplessly, unable to describe it.

"Boom," he said simply.

Yes. That said it.

"We're falling in love," he said, the words sounding like a warning. He turned around and leaned beside her, arms folded, as the coffeepot began to drip fresh, hot coffee into the carafe.

"No, we're not," she denied. "It's lust. We're stuck here alone at a traumatic time for all of us."

"You said it was art," he argued.

"Well, art is full of lustful subjects."

He gave her a condemning side glance. "I think the artist is full of something, too."

"Trevyn, do you *want* to be in love with me?" she asked intrepidly, prepared to hear the worst because she knew the worst was really what was best for them.

"No," he said, and despite the pinch of pain it caused her, she felt exultant. Yes! That was the only way they could go on.

And then he sold her out.

"But what I want doesn't seem to matter," he said calmly. "I am in love with you."

She stared at him, her mouth agape.

He closed it for her with the knuckle of his index finger. "Hey, you and I have a policy of being honest with each other. I'm just being true to it."

That was what she'd wanted. Athena had lied—or to use her word *fibbed*—to David about several things and it had made their lives difficult on several fronts.

But Alexis believed in the purity of the truth. However much it hurt or whatever problems it caused, in the end it was the best recourse.

Or, so she'd thought.

"Well, *I'm* not in love with *you!*" she said hotly, because it was more expedient, more palatable, more…oh, hell. "All right, I *am* in love with you but I don't like it!"

"That's okay. Neither do I."

She repeated his admission to herself and realized she had to have clarification.

"You don't like that you're in love with me, or you don't like that I'm in love with you?"

"Neither one."

"So…" She stood away from the counter and turned to him, opening both arms as though to try to embrace the concept. "It's not a problem for us, then, right? If we don't like that we're in love and we wish we really weren't, then why don't we simply act as though we're not?"

He narrowed one eye as she spoke as though trying hard to grasp what she said.

She hoped he didn't ask her to repeat it.

"I wouldn't be so jubilant," he said, straightening away from the counter as the coffeemaker gurgled and choked the last drop into the carafe. He reached up for clean cups. "You said it yourself. It leaps out at us without warning and we're powerless to stop it."

"It's just mind over matter," she said didactically.

He poured coffee. "Yeah, right. Says the woman who had a foot on my knee and the other leg wrapped around my hip."

"It was your thigh."

He leaned over her until they were nose to nose. "Either way, had we been lying down, we'd have been making love."

"Fully clothed?"

"I had my hands too full of you to undress you. You'd have fallen. But had we been in bed…"

"You're determined to make matters worse, aren't you?" she demanded as he handed her a steaming cup.

"How could they get worse?" he asked. "You don't know who you are and I don't know what I want. Except that I want you."

The words had the strangest effect on Alexis. For a woman whose parents had never expressed love for their children, who'd always felt outside the circle wherever she was, hearing a man say "I want you" turned her spine to gelatin and made her feel…hope.

He picked up his cup and tapped the rim of hers with it. "To unsolvable riddles," he toasted. "I'm going to watch the game with the boys."

Suddenly, desperately, she didn't want him to go. "Afraid to stay and fight?"

He made a scornful sound. "Fighting was my life's work, remember? I'm going because in a ball game, at least I know the score."

HOLDEN ANSWERED HIS PHONE Sunday morning, but had no more to tell Alexis than he'd left in the message. "Except that we've eliminated one of the couples," he said. She could hear papers being shuffled. "A pair from British Columbia. They finally checked out. So we're down to two. Hang in there, okay?"

"Okay," she promised.

They ate lightly at lunch, leaving room for dinner at the McKeons.

Sunday afternoon was the homework battle Alexis

had expected. Trevyn had built a fire and Brandon lay on his stomach on the floor working on a book report, Ferdie curled up beside him.

Alexis had agreed to let Brady work upstairs in his room, then went up to find him watching television. She handed him his books and pushed him gently before her down the stairs to the dining room table.

"I was just taking a break," he argued.

"Really," she replied pleasantly. "And how many of the twenty science questions have you answered?"

Foiled, he frowned at her and sat down. "I don't see why I have to do this."

"Brandon wants to be a writer, so he's working hard on his book report," she explained.

"But I'm not going to be a scientist!"

"I thought you were going to be a mechanic."

"I am."

"All of a car's systems are based on science."

"What kind of science?" Brady tried to argue.

"Do your homework, Brady, and stop giving Alexis grief." Trevyn said, wandering out of the kitchen with more wood for the fire.

"But, I don't..."

Trevyn stopped and gave him a look that made him sigh and open his book. Trevyn winked at Alexis and went to stack the wood in the copper box by the fireplace.

Alexis took the boys cocoa and snacks to keep them going, then carried a cup of coffee to the wicker chair in the conservatory where Trevyn read the Sunday paper.

He looked up in surprise. "Thank you," he said. "You don't have to wait on me."

She held up her own coffee cup. "I wasn't waiting on you. I made myself a cup and thought you might like one. Can I have the magazine section?"

He handed it to her and she settled on the wicker sofa with it.

"What time are we due at the McKeons'?" Trevyn asked without looking up from the paper.

"Six-thirty," she replied. "And shouldn't we bring something? A bottle of wine? A bouquet of flowers?"

"Sure," he replied with a quick glance at her. "We'll leave a little early and pick up something on the way."

"Good."

THAT EXCHANGE HAD SOUNDED so domestic, Trevyn thought. Dinner engagements discussed over the Sunday paper, children doing homework in the other room.

It wouldn't do to get used to this.

What was he going to do about the situation with Alexis, he wondered. He'd been trained to make split-second decisions while taking gunfire, and he'd done it. But he didn't know what to do about a wild red-head.

He should simply not think about it, he reasoned, and a solution would present itself. Like the word you couldn't think of that finally came to you when you let it go.

But it wasn't simply that he thought about her, it

was as though she possessed him. She wasn't just on his mind, she was in his blood.

Like Farah had been.

He didn't want to think about Farah. That always brought up the darkness that lived way inside him.

It was a good thing Alexis didn't want to love him. If she did, he'd have to tell her about that dark place where hatreds and bad deeds lay.

And it would have killed him to see that adoring look she sometimes wore for him die in her eyes.

They picked up flowers and a bottle of wine for Peg and Charlie and knocked on their door at 6:29. The boys wore dark slacks and sweaters their mother had finally sent on with the rest of their things just before David and Athena left for New York. They looked like polished images of themselves.

Peg and Charlie welcomed them cordially and led them inside a warm and airy farmhouse with over-stuffed furniture and an interesting collection of appointments, some of them tasteful, and some of them downright strange.

"Wow!" Brady went straight to a horse collar hanging on the wall above the fireplace. Some free-thinker had installed a clock inside its U shape. "Do you still have the horse?"

Charlie laughed. "No, we never had the horse, son. We found it just as it is in the antique shop in town. You like it?"

"It's really great!" Brady was sincerely enthusiastic.

Brandon looked up at Trevyn and Alexis with a grimace.

Trevyn gave him a stern look intended to prevent him from sharing his opinion on the clock.

Brady then went to what had to be the ugliest thing Trevyn had ever seen. It was a lamp standing on a very civilized end table, but it was hideous. A cupid formed the china base and was topped by a wide, silky red lamp shade with a deep chiffon border embroidered with flowers.

"We love to go antiquing," Peg explained, "and our house is full of stuff, so we buy things for the kids. Our boys bought this house together a few years ago, and we're helping them make all the little corners special."

Trevyn watched the love in her eyes when she talked about her children, and was sure her intentions made every corner special, even if the bizarre antiques didn't.

Peg pointed to the horse-collar clock. "I thought we'd put a family portrait there, and move the clock..." She looked around the room for an appropriate spot. She pointed to a bare wall by the door. "There?"

Charlie shook his head. "I don't think you usually look behind you to see what time it is."

Alexis pointed to an empty spot between two windows. "What about there?"

Peg tilted her head one way then the other. "I'd like it, but Dori claims to be making a quilt hanging for that spot. Of course, she hasn't produced it yet, so if we get our portrait first, she's just tough out of luck."

"Or we can hang them one above the other," Charlie suggested.

Peg smiled at him. "Ever the diplomat."

He smiled back. "When you're causing trouble all the time, someone has to arbitrate. Boys, look what I brought down for you."

Charlie produced a large box filled with toys, board games and puzzles. "We asked our grandson, David, if he minded if we let you use his stuff, and he said he didn't."

"David?" Brady asked. "We have a brother, David."

"No kidding? Well, it's a good name, you know. He KO'd the giant."

"KO'd?" Brady asked Brandon. Brandon shrugged and turned to Trevyn.

"A KO is a knockout," Trevyn explained. "Of course, David and Goliath weren't in the ring."

"David was just a little guy," Charlie told them, settling them on a bright rug in the middle of the floor. "But he was a very good person, and even though Goliath was many times bigger than he was, David got him with a slingshot."

"Cool!" Brady said. "But our brother David won't let us have one. Or a BB gun."

Charlie nodded. "Not good to have unless you do come up against a giant. Well, you look through this and see if you can find anything to have fun with while we old folks talk."

Peg served scallops wrapped in bacon and fruit with a strawberry yogurt dip that the boys inhaled while they inspected a collection of miniature cars and trucks they seemed to find fascinating.

Alexis intended to sample each to be polite and found herself "sampling" again and again.

"How's the search for your sister going?" Peg asked when she finally sat down in the chair beside the sofa Trevyn and Alexis occupied. Charlie sat in a rocker he'd pulled up to the other side of the coffee table to be near the hors d'oeuvres.

Alexis explained about the call from Officer Holden. "We still don't know where she is, but we're hoping there'll be a clue where the flight originated."

Peg frowned sympathetically. "It's tough when a loved one is missing, isn't it? We went through that with our twin granddaughters. They were left at the hospital where Darrick is the administrator. It took the family an entire summer to find out where and who their mother was and why she left them."

Alexis blinked. That little bit of intriguing information left a lot of questions unanswered, but she didn't want to be rude and pry. "And now everything's all right?"

"Couldn't be more perfect. Except for Dori."

Charlie sighed. "Peg, would you stop about Dori. She'll find her place."

"When I'm too old to know it. When I'm in my grave and can't go to the wedding or see her babies."

Charlie rolled his eyes at Trevyn and Alexis. "She's a bit of a control freak. Has to know everything about everyone."

"She's my daughter and I love her and I'd like to

see her happy before I die. What's controlling about that? It's just…just…''

"Maternal," Alexis provided.

Peg cast Charlie a superior look. "She understands. Does your mother worry about you and nag you to do what's best for you?"

Alexis shook her head. "My mother never really cared about my sisters and me. But I think you know best what mothering is when you've never had it."

Peg frowned worriedly for a moment, then leaned over to pat Alexis's knee. "Would you like me to worry about you?"

"You can nag me," Alexis returned with a little laugh. "But, please don't worry. It sounds as though your big brood has given you enough to worry about."

Peg seemed to take her at her word. "What is the relationship between you two, anyway?" she asked with a directness that made Charlie cover his eyes. "You're not going to let a good thing languish because of this silly contemporary search for self. This determination to do everything you want to do before you settle down to the reality that makes life truly livable?"

"We're…we're…" Alexis began feebly.

"In love," Peg interrupted. "It's clear for all the world to see."

Alexis looked to Trevyn for help but he smiled and raised both hands, clearly unwilling to be drawn into the discussion.

"You deny this?" Peg asked him.

"Peg, for God's sake," Charlie pleaded.

"Oh, hush." She dismissed him with a shushing wave in his direction. "I'm just trying to get to the bottom of it. Young people never do, you know. They just stay where they're comfortable, afraid of the big decisions."

"I don't deny it," he replied. "But my past is…complex."

"Ah."

"And I'm cowardly by nature," Alexis put in quickly, buoyed by Peg's brief and nonconfrontational response to Trevyn's honest answer. But she wondered what he meant by "complex." "So, I'm just not a good bet for marriage."

Trevyn turned to her at those words, surprise in his eyes as he seemed to analyze her expression.

Trevyn couldn't believe Alexis's faulty appraisal of herself. He'd seen nothing about her that was cowardly, and a lot to suggest she'd make some lucky man a very valuable companion through life.

Just not him. Because of the dark place.

Peg leaned toward them seriously. "I used to be a teacher, you know," she said.

"*Used* to be?" Charlie challenged. "She's still telling everyone what to do."

"Do you want to help here?" she asked, clearly annoyed.

"No," he replied distinctly, "Because it is none of my business."

"Well, that's what's wrong with the world. Nobody makes other people their business." She turned back to Alexis and Trevyn. "I'm going to give you some homework."

Trevyn waited. This woman was as much fun as she was meddlesome.

"I want you to go home and talk to each other," she said. "Because each of you has made a rather brutal and—might I say—*mistaken* analysis of yourself. And sometimes the best way to discover who you are, is by letting someone else tell you what he sees."

"But we talk all the time." Alexis looked to him for confirmation. He nodded dutifully.

"About what?" Peg asked.

"About everything," Alexis replied. "About what we think, how we feel."

"About each other?"

Alexis thought. "Yes!" she said triumphantly. "Just yesterday we told each other we didn't want to love each other." Then she sat back, as though unable to believe she'd revealed that.

Trevyn simply remained still. It seemed safest.

"Why ever not?" Peg asked.

"Because he's complex," Alexis replied wearily, "and I'm cowardly."

Charlie groaned. "See? All you've done is run them in circles. Don't you have to check on dinner?"

Peg studied each of them worriedly, then stood and went into the kitchen.

Charlie rocked. "I'm sorry, kids. She means well, but she thinks she's some hybrid Freud-Cupid love shrink! Dori won't even come home anymore."

Trevyn's mind conjured up an image of Cupid wearing a Freud-like goatee and he began to laugh, unable to help himself. Charlie joined him, but Alexis didn't seem to get the joke.

Chapter Eight

Trevyn looked at the snapshots of the McKeon family that Peg had spread out on the coffee table and knew they'd make a wonderful family portrait. If it were summer and the weather was more dependable, he'd take the photograph out on the beach somewhere, with them grouped on the rocks or around the driftwood that collected near the cliff.

But he'd probably have to do it indoors, in this room rather than in his studio. Or maybe on the porch.

He struggled against a yawn. Peg had stuffed them with a pork roast, scalloped potatoes, fresh green beans, asparagus and homemade rolls. Cake and ice cream for dessert had put the boys into ecstasy, but he was about to expire with repletion.

Alexis had been charming through dinner but had grown quiet since. She'd told the McKeons about David and Athena, about Gusty, and about her studio and her friends in Rome. Consequently, she'd talked more than she'd eaten, so he didn't think she was suffering from after-dinner weariness.

She'd simply withdrawn somewhat and, though she answered questions and smiled, he guessed she was lost to them.

They left shortly before ten with cold pork for sandwiches wrapped in tinfoil and half the cake in a plastic carrier and the rest of the carton of ice cream.

That was how his mother had always sent company off, he remembered. With leftovers and the memory of her openhearted hospitality.

Peg hugged each of the four of them in turn. Charlie hugged Alexis, then shook hands with Trevyn and the boys.

"Worried about Gusty?" Trevyn asked as they drove home through the dark night. Rain spattered the windshield and sprinkled the road as the headlights picked out the center line. The boys sat sleepily in the jump seat of the truck.

"Always," she replied quietly.

"Is that why you're so quiet?"

"No. I just feel quiet."

"I'm sure Peg meant well," he said, giving her knee a fraternal pat. That is, he intended it fraternally, but the touch left him feeling anything but. "Still, I wouldn't take anything she said to heart. Everybody's different. You can't make blanket rules to cover all of us."

"I know."

That was all she said until he pulled into the garage.

"Houston, we have a problem," Brandon said, and laughed as Trevyn turned off the motor.

"What's that?" Trevyn asked.

"Brady's asleep."

Trevyn laughed. "Must have been that second round of cake and ice cream. I'll get him inside."

"He's no lightweight, you know," Brandon cautioned.

"Yeah. But neither am I. You lead the way, I'm right behind you."

Getting a limp Brady out of the narrow space afforded by the jump seat was a problem, but Alexis helped by pushing from the other side. The boy didn't even stir.

Trevyn slid him out and lifted him into his arms, following Brandon as Alexis closed the truck door, then the garage.

Brandon had opened the front door of the house and Trevyn went upstairs with his burden. Alexis was right behind him.

"If you can get him out of his good slacks and sweater," she whispered, "he can sleep in his underwear."

She'd lost her quietness suddenly, and was all concern for the comfort of the sleeping boy.

"I hope he isn't sick during the night," she continued. "What an appetite."

"He's a growing boy. One day he's going to shoot up six inches and this pudge will disappear."

"I'm going to check on Brandon. Do you think Brady needs another blanket if he's not wearing pj's?"

Trevyn checked the flannel sheet, the thermal blanket and the coverlet and shook his head. "He'll be fine."

Alexis disappeared across the hall.

BRANDON WAS ALREADY IN BED, his clothes slung over a chair.

Alexis tucked his blankets in and leaned over to kiss his cheek. "My mom never did that," he said.

"What?" she asked.

"Kissed me good-night."

"Mine either. Some women don't like being mothers," she said. She'd always been afraid she'd turn out to be one of those because she occasionally recognized some of her mother's qualities in herself. And because she knew so little about giving.

But a week of caring for the boys had helped her find something warm and responsive within herself she hadn't been sure was there. Instead of finding the boys annoying and time-consuming as her mother had found her children, Alexis thought them fun and interesting. Even when Brady resisted doing his homework, she found his rebellion more stimulating than aggravating.

Having Trevyn for backup had helped, too.

"Do you think it's us?" Brandon asked. "The kids, I mean, that the parents just don't like? 'Cause the McKeons sure seem to like their kids. They talked about them all the time. And they're so excited about having a family picture with everybody in it."

"The McKeons are special people," Alexis said. "And you and Brady are great. Your mom was just a lot like mine—more interested in herself than in you and Brady and David. But that doesn't have to affect your whole life, you know. You're smart enough to know you have great value as a human being. She's the one whose life is a mess."

Brandon propped up on an elbow. "I know that in my head. But I still wish it was different."

She stroked his hair and urged him back down to his pillow. "I know. I did, too, for a long time. Then I realized that the past is gone and you can't fix it, all you can do is try to make today better. And you know how much David and Athena care about you."

His strong, square teeth flashed in the darkness. "I know. I know Brady and I are really lucky to have Dave for a brother. And I guess we're lucky that Athena doesn't mind that he wants us to live here. Dave's not our dad, but you know it's kind of the same thing."

"You have a great family now," Alexis assured him. "Neither one of you ever has to worry again. And I'll be glad to stay with you anytime David and Athena have to go away on business or whatever."

"Thanks. I'm glad you stayed with us. And I'm glad you let Trev move in. He's great. Good night."

Yes, he was great. Just not for her.

Alexis went downstairs and saw Trevyn cleaning up the rubble of their lazy Sunday afternoon—folding up the Sunday paper, stacking the few cups and plates they'd used.

"Thanks for doing that," she said cheerfully, casually. "I'm going to bed. So, good night."

He'd started for the kitchen, the newspaper under his arm and his hands filled with dishes, but he stopped to look at her at the bottom of the stairs. His dark eyes were trying to read hers.

She made no effort to hide anything, because she

was sure there was nothing there. They'd agreed there was nothing there.

"Everything okay upstairs?" he asked.

"Fine. Brady's asleep and Brandon's drifting off."

"And with you?" he asked. "Everything okay?"

If you discount this quaking inside, she thought. This sudden edgy need to run screaming into the night.

"Sure," she replied calmly. "Good night."

"Good night," he replied.

She ran upstairs.

As Alexis waited for sleep, Peg's words replayed in her head. "…stay where they're comfortable, afraid of the big decisions."

Comfortable? This wasn't comfortable. And she'd *made* the big decision. She wasn't prepared in any way to love anyone.

Then why did she?

TREVYN HAD LAIN AWAKE for an hour, staring at the ceiling, worrying over all the things that were wrong at this point in time and that he couldn't do anything about Gusty being missing, Bram out of touch, Alexis behind some transparent wall where he could see her but never reach her.

But was that because *she* didn't want him to, he wondered, or because *he* didn't want to, afraid he'd reach a woman he wouldn't be able to let go?

He wasn't sure.

He was prepared to abandon the thought until morning, when the doorknob turned and he heard the quiet creak of the bedroom door.

One of the boys? No. They wouldn't be so quiet.

"Trevyn?" Alexis's whisper floated across the room.

That whisper was certainly no call to alarm, so why was she walking into his bedroom at midnight? He could only hope.

"I'm awake," he said, careful to keep the sudden urgency in him out of his voice. "What is it?"

"Can I talk to you for a minute?"

Now he kept the disappointment out of his voice. "Sure. Come in."

The door closed behind her and she wafted toward him, an unromantic column of pink chenille that still managed to move with undulating grace toward his bed. He suppressed a strong desire to grab her and lay her down beside him.

She sat on the edge of the bed, her exotic fragrance enfolding him, and that was somehow even more seductive.

"I couldn't sleep," she said, fiddling with the belt of her robe, rolling the end over and over her finger.

"Me either." He should have moved over a little to allow her more room, but he didn't want to. Her chenille-clad hip was soft and round against his waist and her elbow bumped his chest as she fiddled with the belt. It satisfied his need to touch her without his actually having to do it and possibly frighten her away.

He propped up on an elbow. "Too much pork roast? I think that's my problem."

"No." She turned slightly to face him, her hip

moving against his waist. He maintained his careful detachment with great difficulty. "I was thinking about all the things Peg said. About people today evading the big questions, keeping things where they're comfortable. Is that what I've done?"

He had that sensation again of the earth falling away. He had to be careful he wasn't misinterpreting the question.

"You mean by deciding not to love me?" he asked.

There was a moment's silence. "No," she answered finally. "I mean by deciding to behave as though I *don't* love you."

"Then, yes." He put a hand to the back of her robe and rubbed gently. "But it was a decision we reached together, as I recall. I was in agreement."

"So, are we doing the right thing because we agree?" she asked, her voice barely there. "Or are we helping each other to be cowards about it because it's just easier?" She turned fully toward him, settling even closer.

He covered her hand with his.

"I mean," she continued, not seeming to notice, "I *know* I'm a coward, but you've proven yourself to be a very brave man physically, so doesn't it stand to reason that you'd also be brave in your relationships?"

He squeezed her hand. "I don't know where you got this coward thing," he said, "but I don't get that impression of you at all. And I was brave in my relationships until I got hurt."

"Farah."

"Yes."

"You'll love her forever?"

"Yes," he replied, surprised to hear himself express what he'd just begun to understand. "But like a fortunate time in my life—a good memory."

"Then you're ready to move on."

He was, except for that dark place inside him. It would never change.

"Yes."

She put a hand to his face and it was his complete and total undoing. Every argument he had against what he suspected was coming disintegrated.

Her index finger traced his eyebrow, her thumb touched his bottom lip.

"I want to move on," she said, a small break in her voice, "but my art was the only place where I ever felt real strength, and though that's starting to come back, I'm still not confident of it. I'm not tough like Athena or sweet like Gusty. I've run away from everything and I..."

This time he did not fight the impulse. He wrapped his arms around her and drew her over his body and to the middle of the bed where he lay her down beside him, her head pillowed on his arm.

"You aren't Athena or Augusta," he said, brushing the wild hair out of her face. "You're you, a wonderful and captivating woman. You're kind and funny and you don't let anybody give you grief. I happen to be completely fascinated by you."

Her gleaming eyes widened in the shadowy room. "You are?"

"I am. And I would like nothing more in my life than to make love with you right now." He tuned out the darkness. This was for her. "What do *you* want?"

She looped her arms around his neck. He saw a tear glisten on her cheek. "I *want* to love you," she whispered. "And I want more than anything in my life, for you to love me."

ALEXIS PULLED HIM DOWN to her and kissed him avidly to make it clear that she meant physically as well as emotionally.

He returned her kiss with clear evidence that he'd gotten the message.

"Let's get rid of this," he said, parting her robe and pulling her tightly against him to yank it out from under her.

The cotton of his T-shirt abraded the tips of her breasts and she uttered a small sound of complaint when he lay her down again. But it was only to kneel astride her and pull his shirt off.

The feel of his bare chest against hers was even more delicious as he rolled them to lie on his back and hold her against him.

She wasted one moment wondering how she could have *not* wanted this, then realized that was silly now that she had it. His body against hers was all warmth and rightness and she felt suddenly as though she'd been fine-tuned and music was coming in loud and clear.

His hands roamed, stroked, swept, explored. She hardly recognized her own body as it came alive and responded. It trembled and flamed and longed for his invasion.

She stroked a hand down his chest, and met the obstruction of the elastic waistband of his briefs.

Remembering the efficiency with which he'd dispensed of her robe, she tucked her fingers inside the elastic and sat up to draw them down.

"Now that was very competent," he praised her as she tossed them over the side.

She touched him and rendered him speechless.

A MAN WAS TAUGHT as a boy to protect his manhood, but at that moment Trevyn would have happily put himself into her permanent care. But he couldn't let that go on right now or there wouldn't be time for all the plans he had for her.

He rolled them again, silenced her protests with kisses, and when she opened for him, running her hands up his chest to his shoulders and pulling him down, he entered her with care.

Her body tightened on him. He moved gently inside her, curbing his desire to allow her time to catch up with his desperate need for her. But she surpassed him almost immediately. He heard her gasp, felt her fingers clutch his shoulders, then her tiny convulsions.

She tried to say his name, but the syllables broke and she gasped again, holding on to him as though the forces of heaven tried to separate them.

As her body trembled, it tightened on him further and he lost awareness of everything but the fact that their hearts thumped in unison—and that their pulse seemed to control the entire planet—possibly even the universe.

If she'd considered their kisses art, what was this?

Chapter Nine

Alexis awoke wrapped in Trevyn's arms—her back against his chest, her hips and her legs spooned by his. Rain drove against the windows and the wind howled through the woods behind the house.

The last thing in the world she wanted to do was move.

Their lovemaking had gone on for some time, she claiming control, then he reclaiming it until they finally collapsed together in the middle of the bed in shared exhaustion.

Her body ached everywhere, but her heart was bursting with newness, with excitement and anticipation. Everything seemed possible. They would find Gusty. They would be happy together. She could come home again to the United States. David's book would be a bestseller. Athena would open a flourishing law office in downtown Dancer's Beach. Brandon and Brady would never feel insecure again. And if she thought really hard, she might even be able to do something about global warming.

Trevyn stirred. His arms tightened around her and she felt his lips at her ear.

She tightened her arms around his. "What a wonderful way to wake up," she said lazily.

"Just what I was thinking." His voice was deep and sleepy. "You kept me up until well after three."

"I tried to go to sleep at one-thirty." She giggled at the memory of his tender nibbling assault on her shoulder, her laughing turn into his arms that had placed her breast where her shoulder had been. He'd reacted and she'd awakened instantly.

He nuzzled under her hair and kissed the back of her neck. "You didn't try very hard."

She shrugged her shoulder against the tickling sensation. "You had a good argument against it." She sniffed the air suddenly as she became aware of the smell of bacon frying.

"Do you think the boys are cooking?" she asked, sitting up worriedly.

He pulled her back to the pillow. "Dotty's back today. Want to shower with me?"

She did, but she had responsibilities. "I have to get the boys off to school."

"Dotty does it all the time."

"I promised David and Athena."

"Then, can you bring me breakfast in bed?"

She hit him with her pillow, ran around the bed to find her robe, then hurried to the boys' rooms. Brandon and Brady were both showered and dressed.

Stunned, she complimented them on their efficiency.

"It smells like bacon and eggs for breakfast!"

Brady said excitedly, stuffing books and homework into his backpack. "Tell Dotty I'll be right down."

Dotty was back in her old routine when Alexis arrived downstairs five minutes later in jeans and a gray sweatshirt. The kitchen clock said five minutes before seven.

The short, plump housekeeper with curly gray hair reminded Alexis of Peg McKeon, not only physically but in her meddlingly maternal attention.

Alexis wrapped her in a welcoming hug. "The boys are so excited that you're back. They've been suffering my cooking politely, but I think they're anxious for the real thing."

"Is there anything new on your sister?"

Alexis related what little news there was as she set the table.

"Sounds as though they're closing in on her," Dotty said bracingly.

Alexis wanted to believe that. "I hope so."

Footsteps thundered down the stairs and into the kitchen. The housekeeper hugged each boy, then shooed them to their chairs, serving up bacon and eggs and toast. She was clearly delighted over their excitement at her return.

As the boys ate, Dotty put more bacon in the pan and frowned at Alexis, who poured a cup of coffee.

"I called the guest house to see if Trevyn wanted to join us," she said, "but I didn't get an answer. Is he at work at that studio already? I know he's always up by now."

"Ah..." Alexis pointed in the direction of the stairs, suddenly pink and tongue-tied.

Trevyn chose that moment to walk into the kitchen, tucking the tail of a blue-and-white-check flannel shirt into the waistband of his jeans.

Dotty looked from him to Alexis, startled.

He went to kiss her cheek. "Welcome home, Dotty. Can I do something to help?"

"No," she said, her surprise changing to a smile. "Thanks, though. There's juice on the table."

"Brady had a nightmare earlier this week," Alexis felt compelled to explain, "so Brandon called Trevyn. Brady wanted him to spend the night, then David thought it would be a good idea if he stayed with us all the time because…"

Trevyn came to her with a glass of juice and kissed her into silence. He put the glass in her hand. "Don't try, my love. Nobody's buying it. Come and sit down."

"Are you guys girlfriend and boyfriend now?" Brady asked, obviously puzzled by the kiss.

"We…" Alexis began, prepared to offer an explanation a child his age could grasp.

"Yes," Trevyn interrupted succinctly. "But that's the only question you have time for, okay? The school bus will be at the bottom of the hill in twelve minutes and you still have to brush your teeth."

"If you had a baby," Brady asked, apparently not having heard Trevyn's statement or choosing to ignore it, "what would it be to me and Brandon?"

"There's not going to…" Alexis began again.

"If you consider my honorary title as your brother," Trevyn explained again, "you'd be its uncle. Otherwise, its friend."

The boys carried their plates to the counter, speculating on that news, then thundered upstairs to brush their teeth.

Trevyn laughed at Alexis's expression and went for the coffeepot to top off her cup. "Relax," he said quietly. "If you tell them what's going on, they'll leave you alone. You dodge them and they'll pester you to death."

"But there's probably a limit to what they should know."

Dotty turned from the stove to smile at them, spatula raised. "I'm interested in details."

Trevyn laughed. "I'm interested in breakfast. You don't want me to report you to Dave for harassment, do you?"

"Not unless you want me to report you to Athena for taking advantage of her sister."

Alexis sighed. "He didn't take advantage. I seduced him."

Trevyn looked affronted. "What?"

The boys thundered downstairs again, ran through the kitchen shouting their goodbyes, then out the front door.

"I went to your room," she said, then added on a note of embarrassment, "just in case anyone asks."

Just in case this somehow caused him a problem as David's tenant, Trevyn guessed. He was touched that that concerned her but was about to deny that it mattered when the telephone rang.

He answered it and instantly recognized Officer Holden's voice. Holden asked to speak to Alexis.

Trevyn hurried to the desk for the cordless and handed it to her while Dotty drew closer.

Alexis listened, then looked both pleased and upset. "Mr. and Mrs. Carter North," she said. "No, that doesn't mean anything to me. Where did the flight originate?"

She listened again, then she said in surprise, "Sacramento! Well, Pansy Junction is just thirty miles from there, but she doesn't know she lives there. Unless she's regained her memory. But, then, why didn't she stay? Why come back through the Portland airport?"

Alexis put a hand to her head as she listened again.

Trevyn rubbed her shoulders, hating that he was powerless to relieve her pain and worry.

"What about the staff at the airport? Did anyone remember them? Did you talk to cab drivers? The car rental clerks?"

She sighed heavily after a moment, then nodded. "Okay, I understand. No, I know it's slow and tedious. What'll you do now?"

While she listened, she gave Trevyn a mournful look. He kissed her forehead and held her closer.

He was glad Bram wasn't here. Not knowing where his baby was would have killed him.

"Okay. Thanks for letting me know. Please keep in touch."

Alexis turned off the phone. Trevyn drew her back to the table and into her chair.

"He said the list narrows down to a Mr. and Mrs. Carter North, for whom they can find nothing anywhere. No DMV records, no Social Security, no nothing. All they know is their flight originated from Sacramento.''

"Near where Gusty lived," Trevyn said.

He sat beside her and Dotty sat across from them, her expression sympathetic.

"You don't think she just went home?" Dotty asked.

Alexis shook her head. "She'd have had to get her memory back to do that, and if she did, I can't believe she wouldn't try to call Athena or me, knowing we'd be wild with worry."

"Oh."

"And if she *didn't* get her memory back, would the 'scary-looking' man have taken her there? How would he know where she lived? Everything including her purse is at the bottom of the river in her car. And why did they come back to Portland? And where did they go from there? The sheriff showed her picture—or Athena's picture—to people working at the airport and no one recognized her."

"Maybe the scary-looking man knew her before and knew where she lived," Dotty suggested.

Alexis sniffed, turning a twisted napkin over and over in her hands. She turned to Trevyn. "I hadn't thought of that. I mean, I presumed he was someone who either came to her aid or took advantage of her amnesia. Do you think it could be someone she knew?"

He tried to organize facts in his mind, but everything was so entangled.

"How would he have found her," Alexis asked, "after she ran away from the hospital?"

"Maybe he took her from the hospital?" Trevyn thought aloud, then regretted it when her worried expression deepened.

"If he was honest," she said, her voice tight, "he'd have just told the police who he was and claimed her. But if he *took* her so that no one would know…"

Trevyn wrapped an arm around her, wishing he'd been less careless. "It's all speculation, Lexie. We don't *know* anything except that they'd been to Sacramento. That's all. He may be some Good Samaritan who found her after she left the hospital."

"Then why did he take her home if she didn't remember where she lived and he didn't know?"

"We don't know that he took her home. Maybe he lives in Sacramento and then brought her back, thinking if he returned her to where he found her, she might remember something."

It was thin, but he thought she was buying it until she turned to him with a doubtful frown. "How likely is that?"

"How likely is anything," he asked, "when we know so little?"

She leaned against him wearily. "I hate this."

"I know. I'm sorry."

Dotty wandered off, apparently wanting to give them some privacy.

"I wish I could think of something worthwhile to do for her," Alexis said, "besides cry."

They sat quietly, listening to the rain against the windows, then Alexis sat up suddenly, her eyes widening. "I just thought of something!" she exclaimed.

"What?"

"I was thinking about Gusty at the airport as the boys saw her, according to what Athena told me. Remember? She was in a long denim coat with the scary guy."

"Yes. What?"

"Well, all our talk about whether or not he took her home made me think. When the boys first told Athena about seeing her double at the airport, Athena had been sure it was Gusty and not me because of her long coat. But David dismissed the coat as a clue because she'd lost everything that had been in the car in the river. And she hadn't been wearing the coat when she was pulled out."

"So, she bought a new one? I know she had no money, but the guy might have bought it."

"But if she had amnesia, would she remember that was her style? I was wondering if the coat means the guy did take her home to get some of her things and that was in her closet."

"But if he knows where she lives, then he knew her before the accident."

"Yeah." Alexis didn't like the facts coming around to that determination.

Desperate to help her, Trevyn had a sudden inspiration. "Do you want to go to Pansy Junction?" he asked.

She sat up, her eyes tear-filled but hopeful. "Really?"

"Sure. Do you have a key to her place?"

She looked deflated. "No."

He grinned. "I have a lock pick."

She actually smiled. Then she sobered again. "But we can't leave the boys. I promised—"

"Yes, you can!" Dotty's voice shouted from the laundry room. "I'm here."

"But the nightmare…" Alexis said to Trevyn.

"I think he's got a handle on that now," he said. "We'll just be gone one night, long enough to get there, look through her stuff to see if we can find anything that could give us a direction."

"Holden had the Pansy Junction police go through the house in the beginning." Alexis said. "He didn't find anything."

"But you're her sister. You might recognize something that would escape a stranger."

She sat up hopefully, drying her eyes with the heel of her hand. "Do you really think it's all right to leave the boys?"

Dotty appeared in the laundry room doorway. "Yes! I promise you I will not let them come to any harm."

"Would you feel better," Trevyn asked, "if we call Dave and Athena at her place in D.C.?" He glanced at his watch. "They're probably clearing out her office right now. You could call there. If we miss her, we'll leave a message and I'm sure they'll get back to us by tonight so we can leave in the morning."

She picked up the cordless again to make the call.

He went to get a cup of coffee, thinking that loving a woman and caring about how she felt was a lot like being a spy. He was working in the dark, the only difference was that in these emotional back alleys he had no reconnaissance to guide him.

Dotty patted his arm as she came into the room to fill the dishwasher. "You're not the footloose bachelor anymore, are you? Somebody lives in your skin with you."

It had certainly felt that way last night. They'd been so close, spent so much of the night body to body that there'd been moments when he'd felt sure they'd morphed into another entity, a real composite of the two of them.

"You're right as usual, Dotty," he said.

She smiled. "I can't believe I've almost got two of you settled down. Bram, of course, is going to be the problem."

Trevyn raised an eyebrow. "Our lives are in turmoil. You call this settled down?"

"This is a temporary problem for which you will find a solution. You always do. And you've finally found what you've needed for a good long time. Love. A loving woman. An obvious gift for fatherhood." She sighed happily. "Yes. Things are looking up at last."

Sure, he thought. If you didn't think about the dark place.

Alexis reached her sister at her office.

Trevyn heard her explain what Holden had found, then their plan for a two-day trip.

THE BOYS SEEMED LESS UPSET that Trevyn and Alexis were leaving, than that they couldn't go along.

"But we could help," Brady argued. "Kids don't

miss anything, you know.'' He added that last, obviously quoting some adult he'd overheard.

''We're like sponges,'' Brandon contributed in the same vein. ''We absorb everything. We might notice something you'd ignore being just an adult.''

Alexis pretended indignation. Trevyn had to laugh. ''You get credit for giving it your best,'' he said as Dotty served dessert. ''But I'm afraid we have to go without you. We're leaving early in the morning, and we'll be back Wednesday night.''

Both boys smiled, but Brady asked with concern, ''Will you have to move back to the guest house when Dave and Athena come home?''

''Yes.''

''But it was fun with you living here.''

''Thanks. I had fun, too. And I'll still be nearby.''

''But what happens when you buy that house on the cove?''

''I'll still be nearby.''

Brady turned to Alexis. ''Are you going to have to go back to Rome?''

''Not for a while,'' she said. ''But it would get awfully crowded if we all stayed here all the time.''

''We like it crowded. Sometimes our mom's house was awful quiet.''

''You sure you guys will be okay while we're gone?'' Trevyn asked. ''You're not going to worry about anything, are you?''

Brady shook his head. ''No. Are you guys gonna have kids?'' he said unexpectedly, looking from Trevyn to Alexis.

Trevyn did his best not to panic.

Brandon, fortunately, came to his rescue. "You're not supposed to ask them that. Sex is private."

Brady was offended. "I asked about babies, not sex."

"Well, sex *makes* babies, doofus."

Brady blew air in exasperation. "I know that. Life is very complicated."

Trevyn heard Alexis's laughter and was careful not to look at her as he laughed, too.

THE FLIGHT FROM PORTLAND to Sacramento was bumpy. Alexis sat by the window, preferring not to look out, a current copy of *Art News* clutched in her hands.

Her tension wasn't entirely due to the flight.

Trevyn sat beside her, by all appearances a cheerful and attentive companion, but she remembered that he hadn't disputed her reply when Brady had asked her if she had to go back to Rome.

As she'd answered the question, she'd half expected to be interrupted by his firm "Not if I can help it." Or, "Over my dead body." Or, "We're going to Rome to pack her things and bring her back just like David is doing with Athena."

But Trevyn had said nothing.

Then Brady had asked if they would have babies, and Trevyn had taken advantage of Brandon's interference on an argument of discretion to avoid replying at all.

She was beginning to worry.

Last night he'd brought her into his room when the house was quiet. Understanding her emotional exhaustion, he'd simply wrapped her in his arms and they'd slept the night through together as though it might set a pattern for the rest of their lives.

He looked and behaved as though nothing had changed after that delicious night of lovemaking, but her mother had often behaved that way, then Alexis had turned to her for comfort or support and bumped up against a cold stone wall.

She didn't think she could stand that happening with Trevyn. So she, too, behaved as though nothing had changed to avoid the confrontation at all costs.

And the issue, for the next few days anyway, was Gusty.

In Sacramento, they rented a small compact car and headed north. From the passenger seat, Alexis watched acres of fruit orchards, rich pasture and grain fields now lying fallow. She knew that nearby on the Feather and the Sacramento rivers men had knelt in streams and panned for gold. Entertainers had struggled to travel to the remote mining camps, hoping to make a living by singing and dancing in makeshift tents to relieve the men's boredom.

Olivia Marbury had been on just such an adventure when she and her three companions had traveled north from San Francisco only to find themselves shipwrecked on an Oregon beach.

"I wonder," she thought aloud, "if Olivia and her friends ever knew that Dancer's Beach was named after them."

Trevyn glanced her way. "I don't know. You'll have to ask Peg McKeon. She seems to know a lot about them."

"It's interesting that it doesn't matter where we go, Dancer's Beach remains with us."

At his questioning look, she realized he had no idea what she'd been thinking.

"Sorry. I was looking at the hills, which made me think of mines, which reminded me that Olivia and her friends were headed to the gold camps of Alaska. I just wondered if they'd worked the local camps, too."

"Reasonable to assume so," he said. "You feel connected to her because of the mural?"

She sent him a smile. "I do. She must have been quite an adventurer in her day, making her own living, starting over after losing her possessions in the shipwreck."

"But she ended up marrying one of the Buckley brothers, didn't she?"

"Yes. I don't know the whole story, but I guess they had quite a struggle at first."

"That's pretty typical, isn't it?" he asked with another smiling glance. "There's always trouble in paradise."

There seems to be in ours, she thought, but kept the words to herself.

Pansy Junction was as small as it sounded, about the size of Dancer's Beach. They passed a small, steepled church, a single-story modern school with a hundred or so children cavorting on playground equipment behind a chain-link fence.

Alexis pointed to it. "Gusty teaches there. Third grade."

"So you told me. According to the police, she

didn't ask for time off or arrange for a substitute, so she apparently didn't plan to be gone longer than the weekend. If she planned to be gone at all.''

"I hope it was just an accident," Alexis said. "I hate the thought that someone would have deliberately hurt her."

The road forked, the right one leading off into the woods, the left curving toward a small downtown area. "It's hard to imagine a reason anyone would want to hurt her."

"She was pregnant," Alexis reminded him.

"Attempted murder would be an extreme reaction to finding out you were about to become a father. And if it's Bram's baby, he'd never do anything like that."

Alexis shrugged. "Keep going. Her house is about half a mile out of town."

"I see the junction, but no pansies."

"They're not in bloom." She sighed. "A lot of us can't seem to get our heads out of the ground right now."

She closed her eyes when Trevyn frowned in her direction.

IT WAS A STORYBOOK HOUSE. The trim and the front door were painted white and, though the contents of the flower boxes were no longer blooming, the plants themselves looked strong and well-tended.

A tidy front porch was also painted white, and a gravel driveway led to a yellow-and-white garage, a square, more modern addition to the property.

Trevyn pulled into the driveway.

"The last time I was here," Alexis said, her voice high and strained, "was when she was named California Teacher of the Year. It coincided with our birthdays and Athena and I surprised her and stayed for a week."

He patted her knee. "You sure you want to do this?"

She heaved a ragged sigh. "Of course. She's okay, just lost, and this is the only way we're going to find her."

"All right."

He had the door open in thirty seconds.

"If your career as a studio photographer doesn't work," Alexis said, shaking her head over his dubious skill, "you can always become a professional lock picker."

"Peg's going to have me take enough poses of her family to pay my rent for the first two months." He pulled mail out of a stuffed mailbox, then pushed the door open and walked into the house.

As he followed Alexis across the room, he saw lace curtains at the windows, antique medallion-back sofa and chairs in dark green, hardwood floors that had collected a light film of dust.

There were drooping plants everywhere, old dolls on the furniture, old toys on the tabletops and the mantel, sun streaming in to give it all a quiet, museumlike look.

There was a drawer open in a small antique desk against one wall, mail rifled through on the table.

Alexis went to it and looked through it. "I know the police have been through all this stuff. They said there was nothing in the phone bill. All the calls were local.''

Trevyn handed her the mail he'd brought in.

There were several local newspapers, a credit card bill from the local department store, a power bill, a picture postcard.

''I sent her this,'' Alexis said, turning it over and frowning over it. Then she sniffed and swallowed and put it down. ''I don't know why that upsets me, but it does. I sent it to her from Provence, grumbling about my problems with my art. And she was...in the river.''

Trevyn rubbed her shoulders. ''You're entitled to your grumbles. Let's check the kitchen.''

It was a large country kitchen with a chopping block in the middle and a small table and chairs off to the side. It was neat, nothing out of place, not a cup in the sink.

Upstairs were three bedrooms, one clearly used as a guest room, the other a sewing room. The third at the front of the house was Gusty's bedroom. There was a novel on the bedside table, slippers neatly side by side by the bed, and a briefcase on a chair.

Alexis sat on the bed with it and pulled out the contents.

''Papers for grading,'' she said, looking through a slightly messy stack of papers covered in youthful scrawls. She put them on the bed, then pulled a teacher's workbook out of the briefcase. She flipped through it and put it, too, aside. Then she pulled out another book. ''*Baby Names for Those Who Love the*

Past,'' she read. She shook her head. ''On the title page, she's written Ethan and Abigail.''

She looked on the brink of losing her composure again.

''Anything else in there?'' Trevyn asked quickly. ''No notes or lists, or anything?''

She turned the briefcase upside down and shook it. ''Nope,'' she said when nothing came out.

Then she peered inside. ''Wait, there's a pocket and something's...ah!'' She emerged with a Post-it note stuck to her index finger.

Trevyn took it from her and read a ten-digit telephone number with a 206 prefix. ''That's Washington, isn't it?'' he asked.

Alexis shrugged. ''I don't know. I wish we knew someone with a reverse directory.''

Trevyn picked up the phone on the bedside table and dialed the number. ''No need,'' he said, winking at her.

''Shelldrake Inn,'' a woman's pleasant voice replied. ''How can I help you?''

''I'm, ah, headed your way,'' he said, making a writing gesture at Alexis. She handed him a pen that had also fallen out of the briefcase. ''Can you give me your address?''

She did. He took it down.

''And what city is that, please?'' he asked.

''Seaview,'' she replied.

''Washington?'' he asked, knowing the woman on the other end of the line was beginning to suspect his motives—or at least his intelligence.

''Yes,'' she replied. ''Who is this please?''

"A friend of Augusta Ames." He forged on. "Can you tell me if she's registered, please?"

He heard the sound of fingers on a keyboard.

"No, she isn't."

"Has she been in the past four weeks?"

More keyboard tapping.

"No, she hasn't."

"Thank you so much," he said, and hung up the phone.

"It's the Shelldrake Inn in Long Beach, Washington," he told Alexis. "The police must have missed the note."

"But what on earth was she doing there?"

He shook his head. "We have an early flight out of Sacramento in the morning. We'll drive to the Long Beach Peninsula and we can still keep our promise to the boys and be home by tomorrow night."

"Should we call Holden?"

"I'll do it. Did she drink coffee?"

"Yes."

"Would you make us a pot?"

"All right." Alexis started to leave the room, then was distracted by a half-open closet. She opened it and put her hands to the soft-colored garments inside. A floral fragrance wafted out as Alexis pulled a flowered jacket and matching skirt out and carried them to the bed. "I'll bring some of her clothes with us," she said. "She'll need something to wear when we find her."

"Good idea," he agreed.

He was told that Holden was out. He declined an

offer to leave a message and tucked the phone number into the pocket of his jeans.

He and Alexis had coffee at the kitchen table and oatmeal raisin cookies she'd found in the cookie jar.

"It's never empty," she told him. "She brings them to school for the children who need cheering up, or who don't get enough to eat at home." She sighed. "I wonder why she didn't tell Athena and me that she was pregnant."

He didn't want to speculate.

"I can only guess," she said, "that it was because she somehow thought we'd disapprove. Which is silly. We all argue, but we try not to judge each other." She smiled ruefully suddenly. "That is, they try not to judge each other. I seem to do a lot of it."

"Why?" he asked.

"I'm hurtful sometimes, because I resent that they're so together and I'm not."

"You mean, because you don't have your art together?"

She shook her head. "No. I mean because my life's never in order." She sighed, fiddling with the hem of the shirt. "Like now. I'm in love with a man who doesn't love me."

The word on the tip of his tongue was a profanity, but he held it back. She wouldn't understand that he aimed it at himself and not at her.

Chapter Ten

Alexis saw that she was wrong. Love was alive in his eyes, strong, defiant. But there was no instant and passionate denial, no rush to correct her. And that was somehow worse.

"I do love you," he finally said calmly.

She decided to confront the issue head-on. She felt coldly calm herself, oddly disconnected. Her sister was missing. Her man was here, yet also missing.

"But you don't want to go that deep after all?" she asked.

He looked down into his coffee, then up into her eyes. "No," he said.

"Then, you're taking back Sunday night?"

He held her gaze, the set of his jaw hardening. "Not a moment."

At the heat in his eyes she suddenly lost the cool disconnection and remembered her complete absorption in him, his total attention to her, and the knowledge that it had changed her forever.

"Then what in the hell was that about?" she demanded, pushing herself out of her chair. Her coffee sloshed on the table but she ignored it. "You said you wanted to move on."

"I did," he replied quietly.

"For as long as it took to get me into bed, and then you changed your mind?" She walked around his chair, then back again.

His eyes were condemning. "You know that isn't true."

"No, I don't know," she insisted angrily. "Because that's precisely how it seems. I sensed it at home last night, and it's been between us all day. I'm thinking happily ever after, and you're thinking, 'how quickly can I get out of this?'"

He shook his head and leaned back in his chair. "Would you please sit down?" he asked with that same annoying calm. "I can't talk to you when you're circling me."

"Is that how love feels to you?" she asked hotly. "Like the buzzards are circling, ready to prey on—"

He caught her hand as she passed him and held her in place. "Please," he said, "if you want to talk, sit down."

She yanked her hand away, snatched a paper towel from the roll under the cabinets, mopped up the spilled coffee and tossed the towel in the sink. Then she sat down and glared across the table at him.

"I'm sitting," she said.

He studied her a moment, as though assessing her ability to hear what he was about to tell her, then rotated his shoulders as though this was going to be difficult and he had to prepare.

She felt a frisson of panic.

"When I said I wanted to move ahead," he said slowly, measuring the words, "I meant I wanted us to have a physical relationship."

"So did I. But it was all wrapped up in my love for you, and an eagerness to pursue a future with you."

That was the hang-up. She saw it in his eyes.

"That's because," he said grimly, "you don't know me. Not really."

"I made love with you," she argued.

He nodded. "Generously. But that doesn't mean you know me."

She made a scornful sound. "That's lovemaking from a man's perspective. From a woman's, it teaches you everything you want to know."

"Lexie, I've killed people."

That statement stunned and silenced her as she was sure he'd intended it to.

"Do you want to tell me about it?" she finally asked.

Now he pushed up from the table, that admission apparently having blown his calm. "No, I don't want to *tell* you about it. It was ugly and dark!" He punched his fist to the middle of his chest. "It's there. It's always there." He paced away from the table, then turned to look at her, anguish and misery in his eyes. "It'll always be there, Lex. Nothing can change that."

"You did it for your country, for—for..." She stammered desperately.

"For all the right reasons," he interrupted. "Yes, I did."

"But, these people you've killed…the world's well rid of them, right?" It was a horrid oversimplification, but she had to say it. "And you didn't just pick them off, did you? You didn't shoot anybody in the back?"

"No," he said, but that knowledge didn't seem to give him comfort. "It was in the course of the mission, to save someone else or to defend myself. But when you've killed someone, you lie awake at night and imagine that target as a baby with everything ahead of him. What happened to him? Hatred? Poverty? Oppression? What made a life so ugly that it generated such ugliness in return? And what has it done to me?"

"Trevyn," she whispered.

"I lay with you in my arms last night," he said, still pacing the room, "and I thought about being with you every day of my life, about having babies and going to church and school and picnics—all the things normal people do." He touched that place on his chest he'd thumped just moments ago. "But I couldn't because it's all so dark."

"Because you've had so much more of that than a real, ordinary life," she said hurriedly. "It haunts you because you're a good person, not because you did anything evil. You'll get over that with time. With love."

"I don't think so. And I can't imagine asking a woman to raise children with a man who's at war with himself."

She looked him in the eye. "Maybe it depends on the woman."

He smiled gently at her while keeping his distance.

"You're just finding yourself," he said. "I don't want to be responsible for turning your life backward."

She could only imagine what that part of his life had been like, but she refused to let him throw away the rest of it without putting up a fight.

She got to her feet. "Well, pardon me, but that ship's already sailed. I *finally* find a man I can love, a man who seems to love me, only to discover that he considers me an inadequate human being."

She carried their cups to the sink and plunked them noisily into it.

He closed his eyes and let his head fall back in exasperation. "When did I say that?"

"Just now. You think I'm not strong enough to put up with your problems without losing ground with mine. What else could that possibly mean?"

"It means that I don't want to inflict mine on you."

"Bull. It means you're too wrapped up in them to let them go."

She turned away from the sink to leave the room, but he caught her arm and turned her around. His eyes were hurt and angry. "That's wrong, Alexis."

She stood still under his hands, hurt and angry herself. "Tell me this, Trevyn," she demanded calmly, though everything inside her was in turmoil. "If you've been so sure all this time that you and I didn't have a future together, why did you make love to me?"

He arched an eyebrow, suggesting, she guessed, that that was a silly question.

"All right," she conceded dryly. "You were desperate for my body. But besides that. You had to know how I would react to it when I've been starved for love all my life. Why would you do that to me?"

His stance relaxed and he ran his hands gently up and down her arms. "Because you have this idiotic notion that you don't know how to love because of your childhood. I know it isn't true. I wanted you to know."

She stared at him as her anger billowed. "So, it was all a lesson in self-esteem?"

He stared back at her, closed his eyes, then opened them again and drew a breath. She presumed it was for patience. "No. It was to prove to you that you have everything required to give love."

She nodded. "But apparently I'm lacking something in the ability to get it back. What good is that? What have you proven to me except that I'm still inadequate?"

His grip tightened on her and he shook her. He was losing it. She liked that.

"God, are you even listening to me! I do love you."

"But you won't show it, so how does that help me?"

"I'll show it," he returned angrily. "Anytime you want."

"Oh, sure. A tumble, but no promise? No babies, no church, no school, no picnics."

He dropped his hands finally and folded them,

clearly trying to distance himself from her. "You don't *want* to understand," he accused.

"That's right!" she screamed at him, suddenly losing it herself. "Because it's stupid. I'd have to have some kind of brain malfunction to be *able* to understand it."

He drew himself up and sighed loudly. "I'm going to the school to see if they'll let me look through Gusty's desk," he said finally, his voice quiet, barely under control. "Are you coming or not?"

"Of course I'm coming," she said, turning away from him to find her jacket and purse. "Haven't you gotten the message that you're not getting rid of me that easily? But I have to water the plants first."

TREVYN DIDN'T TOUCH HER as they walked out to the car, or he'd have throttled her. How dare she misinterpret everything he said, and scorn his altruistic attempt to save her from the darkness inside him.

Being under fire was easier than trying to understand a stubborn woman.

The principal of Pansy Junction Elementary School was a small man with a bald head and a cheerful smile. When Trevyn introduced himself and Alexis, the man was sympathetic and clearly concerned.

"I've never had a more caring or responsible teacher," he said with obvious sincerity. "She never did explain the pregnancy to us and there didn't seem to be a man in evidence but I didn't ask. I couldn't believe it when I read about her in the paper. Her students are putting together a book of letters and drawings to give her when she's found."

"She'll love that," Alexis said, her voice a little high.

Trevyn's instinct was to put an arm around her, but he resisted, afraid it might be bitten off at the elbow.

"We were wondering," he told the principal, "if we could look through her desk to see if we can find anything that might give us a clue as to what she was doing in Oregon."

The principal nodded and reached into his own desk and drew out a key. "We locked it and put it in the storeroom after the police went through it, then moved a new desk into her classroom for the substitute. Come with me."

He led the way down a long corridor. They were halfway along when a shrill bell rang. Doors flew open up and down the hall and children spewed out, running and shouting, separating Trevyn and Alexis from the principal.

Alexis shrank against Trevyn as a screeching group of little boys headed ecstatically for home, oblivious to the adults in their path. He tucked her into his shoulder just before two of the boys crashed into them. Only Trevyn's braced stance prevented all of them from going down.

"Sorry, mister!" one of the little boys shouted over his shoulder as he and his friends kept going.

Alexis pushed away from Trevyn when the hall finally cleared, but not before he was left with the imprint of her body right where his needed no encouragement.

"Thank you," she said reluctantly.

"If you'd been crushed under their little feet," he

returned with quiet sarcasm, "I wouldn't have been able to abuse you as you're convinced I love to do."

She gave him a dark look and walked off toward the door the principal opened at the far end of the hall.

As far as Trevyn could see, there was nothing in Gusty's desk that didn't belong there. Except for a bottle of ibuprofen and a box of antacids, everything pertained to school—supplies, papers, memos, a rubber ball, an electronic game, and several crudely made rubber-band shooters probably confiscated from students.

Alexis picked up one to play with it.

Trevyn pulled out Gusty's month-at-a-glance calendar from the middle drawer. It marked a teacher in-service day and Columbus Day. The two days of the weekend she'd ended up in the river were circled.

"She'd planned to be gone," he said, showing Alexis the calendar.

She took it from him. "Probably to the Shelldrake Inn."

"Maybe. Well, I don't think there's anything here. Let's go back to the house and get the clothes you wanted to bring back for her. Do you want to drive back to Sacramento tonight, or leave early in the morning? We have a pretty early flight."

"I'd rather stay here," she said. "I'm still hoping she'll walk through the door and wonder what all the fuss is about."

"That means we'll have to be up at five," he warned.

"I don't mind."

IF HE MINDED, HE DIDN'T SAY. They went back to the house and puttered around downstairs, still looking through some things. Alexis packed several waistless dresses, found a slip, and didn't know whether to laugh or cry when she opened a drawer and found half a dozen pairs of expansion-front panties used by pregnant women.

She felt a fresh stab of pain as she wondered why Augusta hadn't told her or Athena she was expecting.

On a sudden hunch, Alexis went to the hamper and found it half-full.

Yes! she thought. She considered that conclusive evidence that Gusty had come home after the accident. Her tidy sister would never have left home for several days with a hamper half-filled with laundry.

She pulled out the clothes and went through them, looking for...she had no idea what.

Alexis stared at a pair of denim overalls. Gusty, ever feminine, had always considered them an abomination. Yet here they were in her laundry.

There was a tailored white shirt, a blue-and-white polka-dot dress with an empire waist and a short, flirty skirt. Alexis held it up, guessing the skirt would skim mid-thigh. Gusty never wore anything shorter than knee length.

There was a slim pair of gray slacks with an expandable tummy and a simply cut matching top. The outfit had none of the feminine lines Gusty preferred.

So, she still didn't remember who she was, Alexis thought. Or she certainly hadn't when someone had helped her buy new clothes, as she'd have had to do with all her things at the bottom of the river.

She looked up to find Trevyn standing in the doorway. "What's up?" he asked.

"She's been home," she said, gathering up the laundry and putting it back into the hamper. "This stuff was all bought since the accident, I'm sure of it, and is completely different from her usual style. I think the unidentified scary guy brought her home."

She held up the overalls. "The old Gusty would have never bought these. She was a ruffles and lace sort of woman."

She balled them in her hands and felt something in the front pocket. She dug inside and drew out a flower-shaped opal ring Aunt Sadie had given each of the sisters on their sixteenth birthday. Gusty was the only one who still wore hers.

She felt a wrench in her heart at the sight of it, but refused to let it make her feel worse than she already did.

She passed it to Trevyn. "Apparently, whoever he is, he's making her do the dishes. I don't know why else she'd have taken it off. She's worn it since she was sixteen."

"Friendship ring?" He turned it over in his hand.

"Aunt Sadie gave one to each of us."

"You don't wear yours?"

"I lost mine in a sculpture class and Athena doesn't wear jewelry when she's in court, then usually forgets to wear it the rest of the time." She accepted the ring from him and tucked it into her own pocket.

"So you're sure she was here?"

"*They* were here," she corrected, suddenly finding

clear proof that Gusty hadn't been alone. She held up a dark blue pair of men's briefs.

She sifted through the pile of clothes that remained. "He left nothing else of his. Maybe the briefs being left behind was a mistake. I haven't found any other evidence of a man having been here." Everything replaced in the hamper, she dragged it back into the bathroom.

He picked up one end of it to help her.

"But where would he have taken her?" she asked. "If he brought her home, why didn't he just leave her here?"

"Maybe he couldn't stay and he didn't want to leave her."

"Because she knows something?"

The hamper in place, he leaned against the bathroom doorjamb. "Maybe. Or maybe he didn't think she should be left alone if she doesn't remember who she is. If she can't tell friends from enemies."

"Enemies?" She didn't like the sound of that.

"I don't know, Lex. I'm just taking wild guesses. Let's go get something to eat."

They had sandwiches at a little mom-and-pop diner, stopped at a market for a few things to take back to Gusty's, and Alexis bought a woman's magazine and a chocolate bar.

At Gusty's, Alexis washed the cups they'd used that afternoon, then did the laundry.

She was hanging up Gusty's things several hours later when Trevyn peered into the bedroom. "I'll sleep on the sofa," he said, "if you want to take the spare bedroom."

"Oh, we can share it," she said with an amiable smile. She'd been planning this all evening.

"Pardon me?" he said.

"I said we can share the spare bedroom," she repeated. "I'd even like to make love with you again."

"Really." He sounded suspicious.

The last garment hung, she closed the closet door and gave him a wide smile. "I decided you were right. I wasn't seeing this in the right way. Now that I understand you were inviting me to be your lover and not your wife, I realize I was making a fuss over nothing. I mean, you're a tortured soul and I'm a lost one, and as long as we aren't looking to improve our lot in life, why don't we just hang together?"

She kept walking as she talked and eventually forced him out into the hallway. She caught his hand and tugged him toward the spare bedroom.

"In fact, I've been working this out all afternoon, and if you just think of lovemaking as sport rather than as some heart-to-heart communication..." She turned to him in the bedroom doorway as she suddenly remembered something. "What was that you called it when you thought it was Gusty you'd been with the night of the party? 'That's all love is,' you said. 'Souls touching.'" She waved away that observation with a careless hand. "Well, if you just don't make it all so heavy with significance, we can just make love all night and no..."

He gave her a look that told her she wasn't fooling anyone, least of all him, and turned around, heading downstairs. She reached for the blanket folded up at the foot of the guest bed, grabbed one of the two pillows and carried them downstairs with great dignity.

He was sitting on the sofa, pulling his shoes off.

"Well, you don't have to get huffy," she said, putting the pillow against one end and fluffing it. "I was just trying to be helpful. Boy, give a guy what he wants and what do you get? The cold shoulder."

In a move so quick she didn't see it coming, he put a hand to her waist and shoved her gently but firmly down to the pillow.

"Don't try to play with me," he said softly, pinning her there. "You know lovemaking between us would never be insignificant. That was not what I meant. If I married you, you wouldn't be able to get away."

That surprised her. She studied him a moment, wondering what that meant. "You're presuming I'd want to," she said.

"The thing is—" he stroked her hair back from her face "—if we lived together and you wanted to leave, I'm not sure I could let you. You balance everything for me."

She gave him a superior tilt of her chin. "Then the darkness would be gone, wouldn't it? If I lived with you?"

Looking perplexed and wary, he freed her and sat up. "I don't know. Go to bed, will you? We have to be up early."

She couldn't leave him with that despair in his eyes.

"I have to open out the blanket for you," she said, getting to her feet.

He stood to allow her to do it. "Thank you," he said, as she shook it open over the back of the sofa, tucking the second half of it into the seat cushions. "I appre—"

Finished, she turned to him, put her hands to his shoulders and pushed him onto the blanket.

"What are you doing?" he asked with a quiet groan.

"Providing a little balance," she said, pulling her shirt off over her head.

TREVYN SAT UP, yanked the shirt from her fingertips, and pushed the neck opening back down over her rumpled hair. As he stood up, she looked at him in hurt surprise, her hair caught in the neck of the shirt. A question hovered on her lips, but he didn't even have to hear it.

"Because you're just doing this to prove a point," he said, forcing her arms back into the sleeves, tugging the hem down. "And I have too much respect for our lovemaking to use it that way."

"You used it," she argued hotly, her eyes brimming, her lips trembling, "to bolster my confidence! To…"

He caught her face in his hands and held it firmly. "If you say that one more time," he started to threaten, then knowing he'd never do anything to hurt her, left the threat unfinished. "Your intention is to show me what I'm missing. Probably to make dynamite love to me and fill my head with wild memories so that I won't have a peaceful moment until I see things your way."

She grasped his wrists and pulled his hands down, then folded her arms belligerently. "Yeah. So?"

"So, that's worse than my making love to you because I wanted to prove to you that you're a perfect lover. It wasn't a matter of bolstering your self-esteem, it was because I know what you do for my heart and my soul. And I was sure if we put that together with what I feel for you it would be..." He opened his arms wide, the gesture bigger than any word he could find for it.

A tear fell and she swiped it away. "Well, that was going to be my point."

He reached both hands under her hair, sharply aware of the silk streaming over his knuckles, and pulled it gently out of her shirt. "But I already understand that, Lex."

"Apparently not well enough," she said, "or you'd have proposed to me already."

She stormed upstairs.

He didn't bother trying to sleep, knowing he'd be haunted all night by the point she *did* make.

Chapter Eleven

The Shelldrake Inn was a sprawling frame structure painted dark gray with white trim. Leaded glass windows caught the sunlight, and a cobblestone path led the way from the sidewalk through an herb and flower garden that surrounded a patio tucked in behind a high fence.

Trevyn and Alexis had taken their return flight to Portland, then driven to Washington and the Long Beach Peninsula.

They spoke to each other politely but tersely, last night's argument still like a closed door between them.

The clerk, a pleasant young woman in a flowered dress Gusty would have liked, was reluctant to let them see the hotel's registration book, until Alexis poured out her story of Gusty's accident.

"We're just trying to find out if my sister was here," she said, leaning pleadingly over a deep mahogany desk. "She had your phone number in her briefcase. She looks just like me."

The woman shook her head. "I clerk Monday

through Friday, but I don't remember seeing you— or her.''

Alexis felt her hopes plummet. ''Are you sure?''

''Of course I'm sure. Your looks are pretty spectacular. I think I'd have noticed.''

Alexis didn't notice the compliment, simply tried another approach. ''She might have been here with a man.''

''We get mostly couples,'' the clerk countered. ''What's her name?''

''Well, that's the thing,'' Alexis explained. ''It's Augusta Ames, but she apparently didn't register under her name.''

The clerk nodded. ''A man called yesterday.''

Alexis pointed to Trevyn. ''He did. But you said she wasn't registered. We thought she might have used another name we might recognize.''

The clerk looked as though she couldn't decide whether or not to trust them. Then she sat down behind a computer and punched a few keys. ''What's the date again?''

Alexis gave her the date of the accident. ''But she might have been here the day before, or even several days before that.''

She punched a few more keys, then turned on the printer behind her. ''I'll print out the entire week before.''

In a matter of moments, she handed Lexie several sheets across the desk.

An older couple appeared with overnight bags and Trevyn and Alexis moved out of their way to a sofa across the room. They divided up the pages, checked them, then switched and checked each other's.

Alexis saw nothing in the names to make her think Gusty had been here. She turned hopefully to Trevyn, but he shook his head.

Depression filled her, threatened to overwhelm her. She'd been so sure they had a clue finally, only to have it lead to nothing.

Like my life, she thought morosely.

The older couple registered and started upstairs. Trevyn went back to the desk. Alexis followed him.

"What about the clerk who works weekends?" he asked. "Where can we find her?"

"It's a him," she said. "Paul Crawford. He lives in Astoria."

"Can you give us an address?"

"No, but I can give you a phone number. He's in Portland this week, though. Family wedding, or something."

Trevyn gave Alexis an exasperated look, then thanked the clerk.

They went out to the rental car and sat in it a moment, neither speaking.

"Maybe Holden's found something," Trevyn said.

Alexis scolded him with a look for trying to make it sound as though they had any hopes left.

"If we haven't found anything by next week," he persisted, "we'll make an appointment with Crawford. He should be back by then."

"Sure."

"Something eventually will work."

"Right."

"You're humoring me," he accused gently.

"Only because you're humoring me," she returned. "How long's our ride to Dancer's Beach?"

'Two and a half, three hours," he replied. "We should be home in time for dinner."

She buckled her seat belt and leaned her head back. "That's good. Dotty's cooking is the only positive thing on my horizon right now."

TREVYN IGNORED the subtle gibe. He never expected to be a bright light on any woman's horizon. He'd accepted long ago that his past would get in the way of any relationship.

Or so he'd thought. There seemed to be a rebellion rising in him, a rejection of his noble decision to suffer in solitude and find a way out.

He put it down to temporary confusion. Making love to Alexis had muddled everything in his brain. Everything he'd thought he knew had changed. One moment he felt he didn't know anything, and the next he thought he understood the world in a way he'd never grasped before.

But he was too confused to act. The only sensible thing to do for the moment was coast.

Brandon and Brady were delighted that Trevyn and Alexis were back and met them at the door.

Brady hugged Alexis, then Trevyn. "You're going to be so surprised!" he said to Trevyn.

"You did your homework?" Trevyn teased.

Brady punched his arm. "Not about me! About—"

"Shh!" Brandon shushed him. "Dotty said to just bring them into the kitchen." He turned to Alexis.

"You're going to be surprised, too," he said, but his warning didn't have the delight in it Brady's had for Trevyn.

As the boys led them through the living room and the dining room, Alexis wondered if Athena and David had arrived home even earlier than expected. Or if Gusty had miraculously reappeared.

What had never crossed her mind, was that Claudio would have packed up all her paints and brushes just as she'd asked—then decided to deliver them in person.

He stood beside Dotty at the stove, a wooden spoon in hand as he sprinkled something into a deep frying pan, telling her in heavily accented English, that "marinara is nothing without parsley."

For an instant, all the worries of her life in Dancer's Beach disappeared and Claudio was her reality, bringing with him the old drama and excitement of the studio she shared with him and their artist friends.

She forgot that her art had been in danger of dying, and remembered only how thrilling it had been when her hands had done the work of her heart and her head, when everything she'd felt and intended came to fruition at the tip of her brush.

With a throaty sigh of pleasure, she ran into Claudio's arms.

TREVYN WAS SO RIVETED—so stricken—by her reaction to the preposterously handsome young man with Dotty that he didn't even see the older man seated at a chair at the table until the man stood and the movement caught Trevyn's eye.

The man was a little shorter than he, dark hair graying at the temples, body in brown slacks and a brown and beige sweater, slimmer than Trevyn remembered.

Trevyn felt shock, then guilt, then trepidation.

The man started toward him, arms open, a wide smile on his face and Trevyn walked into Michael McGinty's embrace, wrapped his arms around him and forgot how much he'd once agonized over how this moment might go.

"Dad!" he exclaimed, his chest tight. The man looked twenty years younger than the last time he'd seen him. He held him away to look into his eyes. "You came!"

"Of course, I did. I was so happy that you invited me." He grinned. "Is this young lady the reason? These young men tell me she's your girlfriend, though our friend Claudio, here, denies it."

Claudio held both Alexis's hands and brought them to his lips. "*Cara,* say you love only me!" he pleaded theatrically. "I have traveled thousands of miles to bring you what you asked and I find that you've gone off with another man." He looked heavenward. "*Che dolore!*"

Alexis giggled, hugged him, then turned to Trevyn and his father. "You'll have to forgive him, he's Italian. He's always on stage. Mr. McGinty?"

Trevyn's father offered his hand, but Alexis ignored it and hugged him instead. "Trevyn's told me what a wonderful father he has, but how hard it's been for the two of you to spend time together with his job and your bike trip. I'm so glad you were able to come!''

"I have only two days before a charity bike race in Jacksonville," Michael said. "I have to participate because I've gotten pledges. But I'd love to come back after that, if possible. I can even stay in town if I'm in the way here."

"He didn't ride his bike here, he flew!" Brady informed everyone. "Claudio did, too. For twelve whole hours! With stops in New York and Denver."

"Trevyn," Alexis said, "I'd like you to meet Claudio Fanelli, one of the artists with whom I share a studio."

Trevyn didn't like his looks. He had a Roman coin sort of face, chiseled features, beaky nose, curly dark hair. His handshake told Trevyn he had a lot of upper-body strength, but with all that mouth, it was hard to take a man too seriously.

Though Alexis didn't seem to have a problem.

Trevyn guessed the kid was a good ten years younger than Alexis—and that was something with which the kid didn't appear to have a problem.

What did this mean, Trevyn wondered. A six-thousand mile trip across an ocean and a strange continent couldn't have been taken lightly. Had he come to claim her? Take her back? Trevyn had age and experience on his side, but the kid was a handsome devil and part of the world Alexis wanted so much to reclaim.

"You are the famous boyfriend?" Claudio asked him.

"Yes," Trevyn heard himself reply despite his denials and their arguments over the past thirty-six hours. He didn't look in Alexis's direction. "I'm afraid if you've come to take her back, you're on a fool's errand."

Claudio smiled and squeezed his hand. Trevyn bore it stoically as his bones rubbed together. "But a fool for love, *signore,* is never a laughing matter."

There was a moment of charged silence.

"Dinner's ready!" Dotty announced, giving everyone something to do. She put plates in Claudio's hands, silverware in Trevyn's, a bread basket in Michael's. "Boys, pull the two side chairs up to the table, and, Alexis, would you drain the pasta?"

The boys were full of questions over dinner. They interrogated Claudio about Italy and praised his contribution to dinner—the sauce. Trevyn had to admit that it was delicious.

When they'd exhausted Claudio, Brandon and Brady started on Trevyn's father, wanting a complete itinerary from the start to the finish of his year-long trip.

Trevyn listened with fascination as the once office-bound man told vivid stories of lonely days across the midwest, blown tires in the Adirondacks, an accident in Baltimore where he'd held a young man's severed trachea together with his fingers until an ambulance arrived, a convent in New Mexico where he'd sheltered in an electric storm and stayed a week and a half to fix the decrepit building's plumbing.

"But you're a doctor," Brady said.

Michael shrugged. "Plumbing is plumbing—in

people or in kitchens and bathrooms. This bike odyssey has been a life-altering experience. But it's about time to bring it to a close and find something worthwhile to do with the rest of my life."

"I'm afraid this isn't a very thematic dinner," Dotty said after some time. "Claudio arrived about midmorning and volunteered to make dinner, so we got the sauce going and I'd intended to try to find something appropriate for dessert, but then Mr. McGinty arrived…"

Michael frowned. "You should have sent me to the market. I hate being the reason you—"

"You're the reason we're having pineapple upside-down cake," Dotty interrupted. "And I don't think anyone's going to complain about that."

Everyone agreed and lingered at the table another hour over coffee, milk for the boys, and seconds on dessert.

The boys went upstairs to do their homework amid great protestations and complaints until Claudio went with them, claiming to want to see what American children were learning.

Michael tried to help Dotty clean up, but Alexis insisted he relax while Trevyn built a fire.

Trevyn pointed his father to the recliner. "Best chair in the house," he said. "And you can critique my fire-building skills without having to be on your feet. I suppose you've cooked over a fire while biking?"

"A few times," Michael replied. "Mostly by mealtime I was as hungry for company as I was for food." He laughed. "Most of my retirement fund went for eating out on the road."

Trevyn turned to him in concern. "Do you need...?"

Michael laughed again. "Just kidding. I'm loaded. How are you doing? Starting over's expensive."

Trevyn angled the logs for the proper flow of air then stuffed kindling underneath and ignited twisted newspaper for a good quick start to the fire.

"I'm doing fine. I just finished a calendar assignment in Canada, stashed away quite a bit of money when I was working for the paper and..." He'd never told his father what he did on the side, had never been able to tell anyone.

"Spied for the government?" Michael guessed.

Trevyn, balanced on the balls of his feet in front of the fireplace, pivoted and blinked at his father. "What?"

"Well, that was my best guess, anyway," Michael said. "You disappeared for weeks, sometimes months at a time and could never be reached. You'd have been fired from any other job, yet you always returned to the *Trib* without a problem. And every time you came home, some gnarly foreign problem seemed to have righted itself. I'm guessing CIA."

"You're right," Trevyn said in astonishment. "I never imagined that you knew."

Michael reclined one notch in the chair and crossed his ankles. "Does Alexis know?"

"Yes." Trevyn turned back to the fire, prodded it once, then satisfied that it was taking, pushed the screen in place and sat on the sofa. "Her sister—did you know she's a triplet?"

He nodded. "Dotty told me."

"Her sister Athena married my friend, David Hartford, who owns this house."

Michael nodded again. "And the third sister had an accident and is missing. Dotty told me that, too."

"David and I and Bram Bishop, who's somewhere in Mexico right now, were a reconnaissance team. We finally got tired of the life and decided to live like real people."

Michael studied him. "Something went bad on you?"

It had always amazed Trevyn when he'd been a child that his father would sometimes not come home for days at a time when his patients were in crisis, but he could walk in the door and correctly judge what was on Trevyn's mind, what his wife was feeling.

Trevyn told him about Farah.

"You blame yourself?"

"I did for a while. I think I'm over that. It's just that—I don't know. It's complicated." It hurt to analyze what he felt, like prodding a wound with a stick.

"It's standing between you and Alexis, isn't it? Despite what you told Claudio."

Trevyn shook his head over that. "I don't know what got into me. I know I can't have her. I *told* her I can't have her, but I had to act like a bull elk, challenged by another male."

"That's because she *is* yours. What can't be, often turns out to be what is."

Dotty bustled in cheerfully with a bottle of brandy and two snifters and placed them on the coffee table. Then she left as quickly as she'd come.

"Everyone seems determined that you and I have time alone together," Michael observed as Trevyn poured.

"I'm sure that's Lexie's doing," Trevyn said, getting up to hand his father a glass. "I told her that I'd..." Trevyn hesitated, surprised to find himself embarrassed.

"Yes?" his father prodded.

"That I'd been missing you," Trevyn finally forced himself to say. "That I wished I could talk to you."

"You did?"

Michael looked pleased, almost pitifully so. Trevyn felt a painful surge of guilt.

Michael raised his glass in a toast. Trevyn did the same. "To fathers and sons," Michael said.

They drank.

"Dad, I'm sorry I stayed away so much after Mom died." He hadn't wanted to say that, it just seemed to burst from him of its own accord. The brandy already? "It was just so hard for me to see you in pain. I didn't have the maturity to try to help you in your anguish."

"No, son, I—"

Trevyn halted him with a raised hand and went on.

"Even when I was mature enough to understand, I figured you probably didn't want to see me when

I'd been so careless of your grief. I was proud of you when you took off on this trip, but it was just one more separation and this time it was me needing you, wishing I'd done everything differently. When Farah died I finally realized what you'd been through with Mom, but I had my friends to help me.''

Michael closed his eyes. ''Friends tried to help me, but for a long time I didn't want comfort, I didn't want to get over it because the pain was all I had left.'' He opened his eyes again and turned to Trevyn with a thin smile. ''I've felt guilty all this time, too, because I hadn't done much to help you get over your mother's death. I'd been so involved with my own pain. When you graduated from college and took off to take photographs, I was glad you had your own life, the strength to find your own way. When you went to work for the paper I took such pride in your photos. You have a heart in your camera.''

Trevyn listened to his father's claim of guilt in disbelief. ''I understood your grief. I just didn't know what to do for you. But I never felt that you'd shorted me as a father. I have such good memories of our times together. Of our family.'' Trevyn's voice broke on the last word and his father drank hastily.

''Well, thank you for that,'' he said finally. He smiled at Trevyn. ''You also have a heart on your sleeve, son. Is the memory of Farah between you and Alexis?''

Trevyn shook his head, wondering how he could possibly explain the darkness. As much as he hated to, he closed his eyes and tried to explore it in order to put it into words.

Then he opened his eyes in complete astonishment when he realized it wasn't there.

He tried again.

It was the turbulent events of the day, he told himself—the trip to the peninsula, his father's appearance, Claudio. He was out of touch with himself.

Still he tried to explain.

"I've done a lot of awful things," he said. "And sometimes they haunt me."

"You did them for your country," his father defended.

Trevyn nodded. "That's what Alexis said. But that doesn't always help when I remember the human beings."

"It's to your credit that you remember," Michael said. "I'm sure peaceful means were attempted first before you and your team were sent in. Trevyn, don't torture yourself unnecessarily."

"I guess I'm just afraid," he said, realizing this himself for the first time, "that one day Lexie will look at me and she'll forget that it was all justified and think of me as a murderer."

His father made a scornful sound. He pulled back the lever to lower the recliner's footrest, got to his feet carefully, holding his brandy aloft, and went to sit beside Trevyn on the sofa.

"Dotty says the girl adores you. And though she looked mad at you when you challenged Claudio, it was the kind of mad your mother had in her eyes when I'd bested her. Trevyn, anyone who knows you at all sees a good-hearted man."

Trevyn forced a smile for his father's benefit, then

turned the conversation to the Bikes for Charity benefit.

He knew Alexis didn't see a good-hearted man. She saw a man who'd made love to her for what she was sure were his own purposes, then refused to consider a permanent relationship between them.

She probably looked at him and saw a rat.

At least that was the impression he got when she and Claudio emerged from the kitchen, talking and laughing, and went to the closet for their jackets.

She pulled on a hooded all-weather jacket she wore everywhere, but Claudio had only a fashionable, thin windbreaker with a hand-painted design on one side of the front.

"We're going to walk on the beach," she said, a little defensively, Trevyn thought.

"Claudio, you might want to borrow my jacket," Trevyn said, doing his best to appear unaffected by the jealousy that was like a wolf in his gut. "It's cold on the beach. It's the dark blue one right beside Lexie's."

"No, thank you, *amico*," Claudio replied with a sweep of his arm, as though he were playing to a packed house. "My friend. I am Italian. We are warmed from inside."

"You're sure, Claudio?" Alexis persisted. "It's October. The weather…"

Claudio went to the front door and opened it for her. "I'm sure, *cara*. I will be with you. Even if the snow fell, I would be warm."

Alexis laughed.

"Got a flashlight?" Trevyn asked. He pointed toward the shelf in the closet. "Dave keeps one in the corner. The beach is pretty dark."

Alexis stood on tiptoe and snagged it, then turned it on to test the batteries. "Got it, thanks," she said, and walked out the door. Claudio waved, then closed it behind him.

Trevyn wanted to shout that the Oregon Coast was not the Mediterranean, but he changed his mind, certain Claudio had ears only for the sound of Alexis's voice.

"Well, he's got a line that won't quit," Michael said to Trevyn. "You going to let him get away with that?"

"For the moment." Trevyn took a long swig of brandy, trying to drown the jealousy. "So you're flying back the day after tomorrow?"

Michael nodded. "I have to participate in the race, then I have a few friends I promised to spend some time with, but I'd like to stop by again afterward, if that's all right."

"That's more than all right."

"You think you'll have Alexis walking on the beach with *you* by that time?"

Trevyn couldn't see that far ahead. "I hope a lot of things are different by then," he said. "You're going back home?"

"I don't know." His father leaned back and stared into the fire. "Actually, I was thinking of starting over someplace new. Just like you've done."

"Really. Where?"

"I'm undecided. Cynthia thinks I should stay with

her in North Carolina for a while and see how I like it there.''

Trevyn was surprised. Cynthia Navarro was a friend of the family and the widow of a Puerto Rican golf pro who left her a bundle.

''You two have kept in touch?'' he asked.

Michael nodded. ''She met me in Richmond and rode with me to Charlotte.''

''You're kidding!''

''No. She traveled the circuit with Duardo and kept in shape herself. She's very active. Very active.''

Something about the way his father said that made Trevyn turn to him, wondering if he'd correctly understood that inflection.

Michael smiled. ''I'm very much alive, son. And this trip has done a lot to make me see how much there is to enjoy. Of course, if I had the prospect of grandchildren, I could be lured to settle somewhere on the Oregon Coast.''

Trevyn elbowed him. ''And deprive Cynthia?''

Michael waggled his eyebrows. ''I just might be able to charm her into coming along.''

ALEXIS AND CLAUDIO WALKED hand in hand on the beach, old friends connected by a love of art and their reunion in this place so unlike their sunny Mediterranean studio.

''When are you coming back, Alexis?'' he asked as they strolled under a crisply edged quarter moon. Water rushed and retreated, slapping against a handful of rocks strewn into the ocean by some long-ago eruption. The wind blew and Claudio hunched deeper into his jacket.

"Not before we find my sister," she replied, lighting their path with the flashlight. The moonlight helped a little, but there was driftwood all over the beach, waiting to snag a pant leg or trip a careless step.

"Our studio is not the same without you. When you open the boxes I brought, you will find one from Angelica filled with Grostoli. Everyone misses you."

Angelica de Angelo was the silversmith who'd shared their studio and made Alexis's silver ring. Angelica knew Alexis was addicted to the crisp little cookies she'd often brought to the studio.

She squeezed his hand. "Thank you, Claudio. But I think my life is changing. It may be time for me to stay home."

Claudio's voice took on a dry note. "The man with whom you went to California makes you do this?"

She sighed and looked up at the sky, inhaled the night wind and hoped the fresh oxygen would provide enlightenment. "No. It's my own decision. I think I'll paint here for a while. My other sister and her husband will be back soon, and we've all been apart for so long."

"But art does not flower when it is all—" he made a compressing gesture with his hands "—all tied up!"

"Pablo Picasso said that art is the lie that makes us realize the truth." She tucked her arm in his as they went on. "When you're very young, you can give your all to art, and it's right to do that, to help you find it. But when you're older, unless your art is all you'll ever want, you have to create a life outside of it and fill it with people who mean as much to you as the work you create.''

Claudio stopped, took the flashlight from her and held it under her chin to illuminate her face. ''Are you telling me you are 'older'?'' he asked in disbelief. Then he moved the flashlight so that he could look into her ear. ''There must be something wrong in your brain, *cara*. Let me see if I can...''

Alexis laughed and reclaimed the flashlight. ''You are very silly. I will be thirty soon, Claudio, and while that is still young, it is too old to live only for myself.''

''It *is* the big, moody man.''

It is, Alexis silently agreed, but he doesn't think so. ''It's me, my friend. I have to stop running.''

''Running?''

''Trying to escape, to be free, to fail unseen.''

''Free of what?'' he asked in exasperation. ''Fail at what? You speak in riddles.''

The beam of the flashlight picked up a thick log halfway up the beach. Alexis tugged him toward it and they sat, but found it too bumpy for comfort. They shifted onto the sand and used it for a backrest. Alexis turned off the light.

''My sisters are very clever and I've always felt I was not,'' Alexis explained. ''I moved to Rome so that I could paint and not be judged on their terms.''

''But you are you,'' he said with uncanny perception. ''Who would do that to you?''

''I've just begun to realize,'' she said, ''that I've

done it to myself. I'm the one who considers myself inferior. Well, my mother did, too, but I didn't believe her about anything else, so why should I have believed her about that?''

Claudio put an arm around her and squeezed. "Come back with me, *dolcezza.*" He breathed the suggestion into her ear. "Sweetheart, I know the great prize you are. And art is everything to me, so you will not have to put it second. We will live and love and make art together in the sunshine, not in this cold and windy place.'' He made a dramatic shuddering sound.

Alexis hugged him, appreciating his declaration but knowing that, as often happened with Claudio, the moment had overtaken him.

"Things are not going well with Giulia?" she guessed.

He dropped his arm from her and growled, "She is engaged to Ponti."

"Oh, no. Have you tried to talk to her?"

He raised both palms to heaven in an extravagant gesture of helplessness. "What can I tell her? If she does not love me, she does not love me and there is nothing I can do.''

"Does she know *you* love *her,* is the question, Claudio. When I saw the two of you together, you treated her like a sister. And when she came back from New York, you were surprised by how much she'd changed, and before you could decide how to behave with her, Ponti moved in. It's entirely possible that she prefers you but has no idea how you feel.''

"She is engaged. She must know how she feels about Ponti to promise herself to him."

"She's very young. And an engagement is not the same as a marriage. It's a time to decide if you are indeed in love. And sometimes people find that they aren't."

He absorbed that information then turned to her with a sheepish smile she saw even in the frail light of the quarter moon. "It would be easier if you would marry me."

She hugged him again. "Unfortunately for us, the easiest things are not always the best for you. You will fly home tomorrow and tell Giulia how you feel."

Alexis got to her feet and offered a hand to Claudio.

"And what if she says she does not love me?" He took her hand and pushed himself off the sand with the other.

"Then you will recover," she promised, turning on the flashlight and lighting the path home, "and you will live to one day find another woman whom you can love."

"You are heartless, Lexia," he said, falling into step beside her. "By then you will be married to the big, moody man."

"No. He doesn't want to marry me."

"Why not?"

"Oh, many reasons." They walked some distance down the beach, headed toward the stairs hewn into the cliff, pipe railings affixed to the ocean side. "He did secret work for the government, dangerous work gathering evidence on terrorists and others with plans to harm our country.''

"A spy?" he asked in a whisper.

"Yes," she replied. "Sort of. Anyway, he had to do some things he now finds difficult to live with.''

"Ah," Claudio said, as though it was all suddenly clear. "It is more that he does not want *you* to live with it.''

She stopped and turned to him in surprise. "How do you know that?''

He frowned at her, obviously surprised she didn't. "It is the way a man who loves a woman would think.''

"But I told him that I love him, and I *can* live with it.''

"All the more reason, " he replied. "He thinks you will make yourself do it because you love him, but you will not be happy.''

"Well—but, I…!'' She finished on a gasp of pure exasperation. "How do I fight that?''

He patted her cheek. "Now that you know you are as clever as your sisters, you will think of something.'' He caught her hand and pulled her toward the stairs. "Now, please. Get me out of this frigid night.''

"You should have borrowed Trevyn's jacket," she scolded gently.

He laughed. "I was afraid I would not fill the shoulders.''

Alexis gave him a friendly shove and he laughed again.

Men, she thought, were crazy people!

Chapter Twelve

Dotty saw that Claudio and Michael had everything they needed to be comfortable, while Alexis checked on Brandon and Brady. They'd finished their homework and had changed for bed when she knocked on Brandon's door and was invited in. She was surprised to find Brady sitting with Brandon on Brandon's bed. Brady, less tidy than his brother, was usually not allowed in.

"Everything okay?" she asked.

"Depends," Brandon replied. "Are you going back to Rome with Claudio?"

She went to turn back the bedspread and plump the pillows. "Of course not. What gave you that idea?"

"You went off with him," Brady replied. "In the dark."

"He's my friend." Alexis took a stack of books off the bed and put them on a nearby chair. "That's all. And I'm not going anywhere until we find my sister."

Brandon backhanded Brady on the arm. "Told ya. She's still Trev's girlfriend."

"Then why is Trev so grumpy?" Brady asked.

Alexis raised an eyebrow. "What do you mean?"

"I went down for a glass of milk and asked him where you'd gone. He said you'd gone for a walk and I should be more concerned about my homework than your...what was it?" he asked Brandon.

"Shenanigans," Brandon replied. "What are those, anyway?"

"It's like playing around," she explained, feeling her temperature rise. "Only for a sneaky reason."

Brady thought that over. "You're not like that."

"Thank you," she said, pointing him toward the door. "Trevyn was wrong. It's getting late, guys. Off to bed."

Alexis tucked Brandon in, turned off his light, then crossed the hall to do the same for Brady.

"Trevyn usually knows everything," he said, clearly mystified by the turn of events. "I wonder what he meant."

"I haven't a clue." She tucked the blankets in around his neck and turned off the light.

"I bet he just didn't like it," Brady's voice said in the darkness, "'cause you went out with Claudio."

"Good night," Alexis said, pulling his door closed.

She almost collided with Trevyn.

"Full house tonight," he said without expression. He pointed down the hall. "My dad's in Dave and Athena's room."

"Good," she said. "He should be comfortable there." She pointed to her own room. "I'll be in mine, if you'd like to check it occasionally for *she-nanigans.*" She emphasized his word.

He looked more resigned than embarrassed that his remarks had been passed on to her. "Good thing I'm no longer an agent. No such thing as confidences around here."

"Oh, yeah," she said, irritated that he didn't even have the grace to be embarrassed, "well, next time you talk to the boys about me, I'd appreciate it if you didn't malign me."

He looked offended. "Malign you?"

"Shenanigans," she said, folding her arms, "suggests high jinks for the purpose of deceit. I have never indulged in shenanigans."

"Never?" He brushed something off the shoulders of her jacket, then turned her around and brushed between her shoulder blades. "Then how'd you get sand all over your jacket?" He swiped once at the seat of her pants. "And on your backside?"

"We were sitting," she began to explain before her annoyance caught up with his nerve in asking the question. "What the hell business is it of yours?" she demanded.

He shushed her and pulled her toward the stairs. "Keep your voice down," he admonished. "You want to bring everyone out into the hallway?"

"Why not?" she asked, voice still at full volume. "Maybe we could take a vote on whether or not everyone thinks I indulged in shena—!"

He covered her mouth and drew her halfway down the stairs before lowering his hand. "What is the matter with you?"

"With me? You're the one who doesn't want anything to do with me but seems to think you still have a right to monitor my behavior!"

"I wasn't monitoring," he corrected darkly. "I was simply observing."

"And misinterpreting everything as usual. God! I've never seen a man so equipped to be wonderful, but so determined to be *wrong* instead. You will do yourself a great service if you just steer clear of me, McGinty. Permanently!"

Alexis ran up the stairs to her room and closed herself in.

TREVYN AND MICHAEL DROVE Claudio to the airport the following morning. Trevyn didn't want to like him, but the expansive Italian had a charm that was hard to ignore. Since he was leaving, Trevyn decided he could be generous.

He talked for one hundred miles about the studio in Rome, about their friends, their communal lunches, their late nights in the summer with Luciano and Laura's children sleeping all around them.

He gave his address to Michael, who promised to look him up if he decided to motorcycle through Europe. "Not a wise way to travel in Italy," Claudio said. "The Alps, the hills. You will be old before your time."

Claudio bought them coffee at the airport, and they walked him to his gate.

Claudio drew Trevyn aside.

"My father," he said, large dark eyes suddenly without their usual light, "is a mafioso."

Trevyn was stunned by the quietly spoken revelation.

"He has terrified, hurt, maimed, murdered those who have tried to stop him, those who won't pay what he asks, those who cannot repay what he lends. Those who fail him."

Trevyn remained speechless while Claudio drew a broken breath. "*That* is a murderer, not you. That is a man with whom a woman could not stay. Over whom a woman would throw herself from the steeple of a church when she learned what he did."

"Claudio..." Trevyn put a hand to his arm at the stricken look in his eyes.

Claudio smiled, suggesting his sympathy was unnecessary.

"Our priest found me a family," he said, his tone suddenly lighter, "who had four other children, and I was raised like one of theirs. I was very happy. And now I make art to put good in place of the bad—in the world, in my heart."

Trevyn was first astonished then humbled by the young man's old wisdom—and his generosity.

Claudio tapped the patch of jacket over Trevyn's heart with his index finger. "Alexis will put good in there for you. But you have to make room."

The flight was called and there was a sudden flurry of activity as people rose and formed a line. Trevyn wrapped Claudio in a bear hug, then shook his hand.

"Safe trip home," Trevyn wished him.

Michael said goodbye, then Trevyn felt compelled to watch at the window until the flight took off. His father didn't ask why.

ALEXIS TOOK A CAB to the studio with her paints and supplies after the boys left for school and the men left for the airport. She'd hugged Claudio, wished Michael a good day exploring Portland, and gave Trevyn a stiff goodbye.

It was clear that things weren't going to work out between her and Trevyn and she could think of only one way to get him out of her system. She should be working on the mural today, but she had to do this for herself.

There was nowhere to paint at home, but she'd decided that the back room of Trevyn's studio would be perfect for her project. It had been cleaned but not painted yet and she would be alone in it all day.

She tacked a four-by-five-foot length of canvas to the wall and stood back to make sure it was taut. There was no time to prime the canvas, but she wasn't after archival-quality work here, just the simple release of getting Trevyn out of her system.

She'd learned in art school that a large work surface encouraged scope, discouraged smallness of thought or technique.

With cerulean blue, she made her first few strokes, the beginnings of the contours of a face.

She worked with coffee in one hand and the brush in the other.

Dotty had made her a ham and cheese on rye for lunch and she ate that while struggling with the tilt of Trevyn's right eyebrow.

Midafternoon the coffee shop delivered a double tall, double shot hazelnut mocha and a biscotti. They got her through to the final spot of light in the pupil of his right eye.

She dropped her brush in the can of turpentine and stepped back to the opposite wall.

She was good. She was *back!* It was in some ways the most traditional thing she'd ever done, but also the most satisfying. She always prided herself on her skewed vision of what she saw, but this was representational art at its sharpest—and probably the most surreal thing she'd ever done, considering the state of their relationship.

She dusted her hands off. Done. Finished. Trevyn McGinty out of Alexis Ames's system once and for all.

She washed her brushes, packed up her paints, called a cab and went home in time to have dinner with Dotty and the boys.

"WANT TO SEE MY STUDIO?" Trevyn turned onto Dancer's Avenue, the old streetlights illuminating the quiet downtown. At just after eight o'clock Dancer's Beach was buttoned up tight, a light on in every shop for the cop on the beat, but not a car on the street, except for one in front of city hall.

"I'd love to," Michael said on a groan. "And then I think I'll jog home behind the car. After lunch at Jake's, coffee and Cinnabons at the mall, and that Mexican feast tonight, the new shirts I bought to visit Cynthia aren't going to fit me."

"You'll work it off on the bike benefit." Trevyn pulled up in front of the building and parked. "Now don't expect too much. The mural I was telling you about is only half-finished, and I haven't even painted my office yet. Some of my equipment's moved in, but I've got it all shoved together under a tarp.''

Michael stopped in the middle of the sidewalk and looked up and down the street. ''This town is like something out of a Rockwell painting. Makes you feel so all-American somehow. Like you'd be willing to die for this.''

Trevyn drew a breath and held it. That was probably why he related so well to Dancer's Beach, he thought. He'd spent quite a few years defending this very way of life.

He unlocked the door to his studio and flipped on the light.

The smell of paint was strong and had a slightly different element in it than he'd grown used to over the past week. Or maybe it was just because the space had been closed up tight for four days.

His father went straight to the mural. ''Talented woman,'' he said, after studying the grouping of women on the far side.

''She is,'' Trevyn said. He'd tried not to think about her today, to concentrate on his father and all he'd wanted to tell him, to do for him.

But her image had been there every moment, her voice in his ear, her touch on his skin, the sad look in her eyes after their quarrel last night imprinted on his brain.

Superimposed on all that had been the memory of the story Claudio had told him.

Trevyn could still feel the tap of Claudio's finger

over his heart. "Alexis will put good in there for you," he'd said. "But you have to make room."

He'd wandered through the Portland Art Museum with his father, he'd taken him shopping, they'd eaten their way across the mall and Trevyn had kept up his half of the conversation, but all the while a corner of his brain had been telling him he'd left it too late with Alexis. He'd seen it in her eyes last night. She'd had it with him. She'd offered him everything, and he'd been afraid he had no place to put it, to cherish it, to care for it so that they could go on together.

But he'd been wrong. He'd grown so used to that dark place inside him running his life, that when he'd tried to explain it to his father and found it empty, he'd been sure he was mistaken. It couldn't be.

Then he'd lain awake most of the night, trying to find it. The memories and the recriminations always came to him at night, but all he could locate were muddled impressions, elusive memories with softened edges. No anger, no hatreds, only spent grief.

Even his thoughts of Farah were the good ones, her laughter, her sweetness, her zest for everything.

Now as he looked at the half-finished mural with its dancers in Victorian dress, looking out at the water, Olivia standing a little apart from them, he understood the poignancy of the work. Alexis had portrayed the women so well because she felt like Olivia—beyond the circle, odd woman out.

And he had done little to improve that situation for her.

Had he lost his chance with her because he'd failed

to see that she'd changed him? That the place where the darkness had been was now filled with love?

It was a startling epiphany. Love. He was filled with love.

Too late?

"Got any clients yet?" Michael asked as he peered under the tarp.

Trevyn shifted emotional gears. "I do, as a matter of fact," he said. "A big family portrait scheduled for the end of this month."

"How many people?"

"Ah…" Trevyn tried to remember, counting. "Fourteen, I think. That includes several kids and lots of babies, so this should be an experience."

His father became pensive. "That's what I always wanted. A big, noisy group." He grinned. "But you came along and seemed to make enough noise to compensate for the rest of the kids that didn't."

Trevyn put an arm around his shoulders and led him toward the back. "I can fuss and carry on for you any time you want me to. This is going to be my of—"

He'd led his father into the room and turned with a sweep of his hand to explain that eventually he would paint and paper in here, when his eyes fell on the giant canvas tacked to the wall.

It took him a moment to recognize himself. The colors in the five-foot high portrait of a face and shoulders were unorthodox. Skin tones using blue, lavender, yellow and rose seemed wrong at first glance, then as his brain interpreted planes and shadows out of the colors, he saw a dark-eyed man with strong features and a wealth of information in his eyes.

He'd lived a lot. He'd seen painful things he'd been forced to deal with. He'd lost someone. But there in the line of a firm mouth, in the angle of a stubborn chin, in a sort of vulnerability in the gaze, was the willingness to try again.

For a moment Trevyn couldn't tear his eyes from his own portrait, and what it suddenly revealed to him about Alexis. But he felt his father turn to him and, with amusement clear in his voice, ask, "Now what is it again that makes you think this woman *doesn't* love you?"

ALEXIS LAY SOBBING in the middle of her bed.

She'd come home from her all-day painting marathon energized, resolved. She'd done the sensible thing. She'd gotten Trevyn out of her system in the way that worked best for her, and while doing it, she'd reconnected with her artistic self. With her personal self.

She'd enjoyed dinner with Dotty and the boys, listening to Brady talk about the upcoming band concert at school, to Brandon explaining an idea he had for a private detective character who was an artist.

"People come to him," he said, "because he sees things in a different way, so he catches stuff that the police miss. And he knows lots of interesting characters, so there'd be lots of fun people to put in the story."

"I think that sounds excellent," she'd said. "What a good idea."

"I think he should have a sidekick who's a photographer," Brady contributed, "'cause he'd be taking pictures all over and maybe he'd get a criminal in the photo, or something, and they'd drag him into an alley and yank out his film!"

As Brandon considered that, Alexis felt her euphoria begin to ebb. She missed Trevyn being across the table from her, teasing the boys, teasing Dotty, making everyone laugh.

She wondered just what it was that made him feel there was darkness inside him. In the brief space of time she'd known him, he seemed to project light— to the boys and to herself.

Despite his denials, it must be Farah. She'd been loving and brave and sure enough of who she was to put herself in the way of what would have harmed her friends and the man she loved.

That was it. He chose to live with a dark memory rather than with Alexis, who couldn't find her art, couldn't find herself.

Ironic, she thought, as she and the boys helped Dotty clear the table, that she'd finally found her art. It had begun to come back in the mural, maybe because Trevyn had been at the other end of the room, whistling as he moved furniture and painted walls.

She knew she'd recaptured it completely when she painted Trevyn's face today. All the emotion she'd lately suppressed or simply couldn't find had surged out of her and into her brush. The force of it had cleared away all obstruction to her creative process and her head was suddenly crowded with ideas, her fingers itching to work.

The only problem was she was just beginning to realize that working Trevyn out of her system was not at all the same as getting him out of her heart.

And as she came to that realization, what was left of her cheerful mood evaporated completely. She managed to help Dotty clean up and get the boys started on their homework just before acute depression took over.

Now she lay sprawled across her bed, wondering too late why she hadn't been more understanding of the time and space Trevyn needed. He'd once said, "You don't know who you are and I don't know what I want."

That, at least, had changed. She finally understood herself, and he now knew what he wanted—it just wasn't her.

She'd learned she was strong enough to accept that reality, she thought, sobbing brokenly into her pillow. But it was going to hurt until the day she died.

She should have gone back to Rome with Claudio. But she couldn't leave until Gusty was found.

She wept anew, wondering how a life she was finally getting together could still be so on its ear.

As she finally climbed out of bed, thinking a shower might help revive her so she could check on the boys, she heard their footsteps thunder down the hallway, Ferdie barking as he followed, then the sounds of a commotion downstairs.

She opened her door a crack, listening for some indicator of what had happened. Was Trevyn home?

She did hear a man's voice, but it wasn't his; she knew every subtle nuance in it now.

David and Athena were home.

Delighted that her sister and her new brother-in-law were back safely, she couldn't help a sense of disappointment that her house-playing days at Cliffside were over. Trevyn would go back to the guest house, the boys would no longer need her, she would be lady of the house no more.

Well, of course not, she told herself as she went downstairs to welcome her sister and David home. *Get your own life.*

There was an entire suitcase of gifts. Baseball hats, sweatshirts, and autographed baseballs by the New York Yankees for the boys; a cotton throw for Dotty patterned with New York attractions, a beautiful pin for Alexis from the gift shop at the Museum of Modern Art.

Alexis hugged David, who was closest, then Athena.

Athena held her an extra moment, then drew her into the kitchen while David showed Dotty the Ansel Adams print they'd bought for Trevyn.

"What happened?" Athena asked Alexis. Her eyes studied her sister's face, clearly seeing something she didn't like.

Alexis felt exhausted, and the last thing she wanted at the moment was to be interrogated about Trevyn. But Athena stood there, bright as a candle, and Alexis suddenly found it difficult to shrink back into her own shadow of hopelessness.

"To put it succinctly," she replied, "Trevyn and I got very close while you were gone, but after we made love, he told me he doesn't want a relationship—that there are dark corners of his soul I won't be able to deal with.''

Athena put a hand to her arm. ''Do you think you can?''

''Of course I can.'' Upset anew, Alexis went to the kitchen table and fell into a chair. ''He thinks he's this bad, dark man and really he's... so kind.''

Athena followed and took the chair at a right angle to her. ''Did you tell him that?''

''Athena, I talked until I couldn't think of anything else to say.'' She sighed. ''The simple truth is that, even if his reason is all wrong, he does not want me to love him.''

''Can he stop you?'' Athena asked with a smile.

''If he won't love me back, he can. I'm just getting over Mom not loving us. I can't go through it again with a husband.''

''So you talked about marriage?''

Alexis made a face. ''No. I dreamed about it while he was wondering how to get away.''

''Where is he now?''

''He took my friend Claudio back to the airport.''

Athena raised an eyebrow. ''Claudio who shares your studio? He was here?''

Alexis nodded. ''He brought my paints and stuff. I'd asked him to ship them, but Claudio's Italian, you know. All for the grand gesture.'' She dismissed the visit with a wave of her hand. ''He's having trouble with a girl. It's all very complicated. But Trevyn's dad is here, too. He flies back tomorrow for a char-itable benefit he's involved in and to visit some friends, but he wants to come back in a couple of weeks.''

Athena smiled widely. "How wonderful. I'm sorry I missed Claudio. But, about you and Trevyn..."

Alexis got wearily to her feet. "That's just not going to happen. And I can live with that...just not happily."

Athena stood and wrapped her arms around her, holding tightly. "Don't let him go, Lexie. He's not Mom. He's just been through a lot and doesn't want to hurt you with the stuff he finds hard to remember. Just imagine what these guys have seen and done while you and I and Gusty were chasing our dreams."

Alexis did find that a sobering thought. While she was pursuing art in sunny Italy, Trevyn was working under very different conditions.

But what could she do, she wondered helplessly, if he didn't want her?

Alexis hugged Athena, then took a step back. "About Gusty," she said.

"Right. You called us from Pansy Junction to tell us you were going on to Seaview, Washington."

Alexis nodded. "The desk clerk at the inn printed out a week's worth of registrations before Gusty's accident and her name wasn't on it. Trevyn and I both checked and there wasn't one name we recognized. I asked the clerk if she remembered registering anyone who looked like me, and she didn't. But the weekend clerk was off that day and in Portland at some family function. She gave us his home phone number so we can call him when he comes back. So far," she added, her voice reflecting the despair in Athena's eyes, "that's our only clue."

Athena nodded grimly. "No word from Holden?"

"No."

David wandered into the kitchen, took one look at their faces and wrapped an arm around each of them.

"I presume," he said, "that there was no good news from your trip to Seaview."

Alexis frowned up at him and repeated the story she'd told her sister.

"Where's the registration list?" David asked.

"Trevyn has it."

Alexis explained about their unexpected visitors, and Trevyn's trip to the Portland Airport.

David kissed Athena's forehead, and gave Alexis an extra squeeze before releasing them.

"I'm glad his dad came," David said. "He's been worried about their relationship. You and Trevyn did a great job with the boys while we were gone. They're pleading with me not to let Trevyn move back to the guest house."

Alexis had to smile at the memories. "The boys are such good kids. We had a great time."

Alexis hugged Athena and David one more time. "Well, if you two don't mind, I'm off to bed."

"Don't forget what I said," Athena cautioned.

David smiled at her. "Did you say something brilliant *again?*"

Athena fluttered her eyelashes playfully. "Every word that passes these lips…" she began.

David caught her in his arms and tipped her backwards with a flourish. "Don't waste those lips on words," he pleaded and kissed her.

Athena wrapped her arms around his neck, he straightened, and whatever frivolous play inspired the kiss was lost in the sudden embrace of two people very much in love.

Her presence clearly forgotten, Alexis left the kitchen and went to bed.

Chapter Thirteen

Trevyn and Michael arrived home shortly after ten o'clock.

"Dave and Athena are home," Trevyn said as he pulled into the garage and saw the blue sedan in its spot. "We'll move into my place, Dad, as soon as I introduce you."

"I hope they're not angry that you gave me their room." Michael unbuckled his belt and climbed out of the truck. "Honeymooners can get pretty serious about that stuff."

Trevyn laughed. "Dave seldom gets angry about anything." He closed the garage and they walked side by side to the house.

Brandon and Brady greeted them at the door. "We all got presents!" Brady said excitedly. With Brandon standing beside his brother, both wearing New York Yankees sweatshirts and hats, Trevyn considered the announcement unnecessary.

"You didn't get anything, though," Brady added

sadly to Michael. "They didn't know you were here."

"I've enjoyed their hospitality," Michael replied, wrapping an arm around each boy as they followed Trevyn to the kitchen. "That was present enough."

David and Athena sat at the table, drinking coffee.

"Trevyn!" Athena stood and opened her arms to him.

Trevyn walked into them. As she wrapped her arms around him and kissed him soundly on the cheek he wondered what mysterious secret David had learned to make a woman so happy.

She leaned away from him, smiling. "Thank you for taking such good care of the boys and Alexis."

"My pleasure," he replied, then felt traitorous for taking the credit. He had done his best with the boys, but all he seemed to have done for Alexis was make her miserable.

But she loved him still. He'd seen it in the painting. He just had to pray that she hadn't reverted to their original plan to behave as though their love didn't exist in the hope that would kill it.

He couldn't think about that possibility.

David came to wrap him in a bear hug. "Thank you," he said sincerely. As the boys went to examine the contents of the refrigerator, he added for Trevyn's ears alone, "I was worried about Brady, but he says you made him understand I'd be back and feel better about our being gone."

Trevyn shrugged as though that was easy to understand. "Of course I did. Poor kids get stuck with you for a brother, I probably seem like Chuck Norris to the rescue.''

David rolled his eyes, then turned his attention to Michael and offered his hand. "Are you responsible for the creation of this windbag?"

Michael cast his eyes down in pretended apology. "Guilty, I'm afraid. I'm Michael McGinty."

David introduced himself, then Athena.

"I'm embarrassed to find that I've taken your room," Michael said. "Trev and I will move back into—"

"No!" Athena said with a firmness that surprised all of them. She smiled sweetly at Michael. "You're welcome to keep your room tonight since Trevyn has to take you back to the airport tomorrow. And, Trevyn?"

"Yes."

"You're not leaving this house until you do something about Lexie."

He smiled blandly. "I intend to, but I'm going to need magic or miracles."

She nodded. "As long as you get it done."

The doorbell pealed loudly through the house.

Trevyn stayed David with a raised hand. "Pour my dad a cup of coffee. I'll get the door." He glanced at his watch as he left the room and wondered who would be visiting at this late hour.

He opened the front door and was astonished to see Clarissa standing there, the collar of a chic red woolen coat pulled up against the chill. Her white hair curled around her head like a halo, and in her hand she held... He looked a second time to be sure. Yes, it was a wand.

The hair prickled along his arms as he remembered his declaration of a moment ago that he'd need magic or a miracle to deal with Alexis. And here stood an angel with a magic wand.

"Clarissa?" he asked in disbelief. "What can I do for you?"

She touched his shoulder with the star tip of her wand. "Actually, I'm here to do for you. Mr. McGinty?"

He nodded. "Yes. You know that's me."

She looked at a note in her hand. "No, I need Michael McGinty."

"That would be me." Trevyn's father appeared beside him. "Clarissa?"

Trevyn watched in complete confusion as they shook hands.

"I apologize for being so late," she said. "But I stopped to see some friends along the way and one of them followed me to drive me home again, but I lost her somewhere on Highway 18 and had to backtrack. I hope I haven't awakened everyone."

Michael shook his head. "I've just gotten home myself."

She handed him the wand. Dangling from it was a key. "Now, I promise you it's in excellent condition, but if you'd like to drive it first, I'd be happy to wait."

Michael shook his head. "Not necessary. My son

was impressed with you, so I'm sure you're a woman of your word.''

''I am.'' She swept a hand behind her and for the first time, Trevyn noticed the car in the shadow beyond the pool of light near the front door.

It was the Duesenberg!

''Thank you, Clarissa.'' Michael walked her to her friend's car, Trevyn following in mystification.

Before getting in, Clarissa patted Trevyn's cheek. ''You should honeymoon in it,'' she said. ''I hope you have as smooth a ride as Henry and I did.''

With all she'd lost, Trevyn thought, she'd still considered her life a good ride. Attitude, he decided, was everything.

Then something else she'd said occurred to him. ''Me? *My* ride?''

''I believe it's a gift,'' she said, and patted his cheek again. ''Goodbye, you gorgeous McGintys.'' She climbed into the passenger seat, and the driver, a woman of similar vintage in a roll-brimmed hat, turned with tires squealing and headed down the driveway.

Trevyn turned to his father, who handed him the wand. He saw on closer inspection that it was a key-holder intended to hang on a wall.

Trevyn refused to reach for it. ''Dad, that cost a fortune! I can't poss—''

Michael grinned. ''Yes, you can. A gift from me to you to celebrate your new life, to help you remember how much you're loved. And when you are loved, you're usually capable of giving love in great quantities, over long periods, until it's a self-perpetuating thing that then sustains you." Michael forced the key into Trevyn's hand.

"But how did you know? Where...?"

"The boys told me about the car, said that you'd put Clarissa's business card in the pocket of your shirt. We found the shirt, I called Clarissa." Michael shrugged. "It was easy. Please. Just accept it as something I could do for you."

Trevyn maintained his composure with great difficulty. "I don't know what to say, Dad," he whispered.

"The words I'd like to hear one day soon," Michael said with a sniff, "are, 'Dad, you're going to be a grandfather.'" He clapped Trevyn on the shoulder. "The sooner you can set that in motion, the happier I'll be."

Michael walked into the house and Trevyn was left alone with the beautiful green and black Duesenberg. *His* Duesenberg.

He pulled the door open and got a whiff of Clarissa's perfume as he climbed into the car. He sat behind the wheel and let the delicious opulence of the classic piece of art envelop him.

He rested his wrist on the top of the steering wheel and began to plot.

"LEX?"

Alexis turned over in bed, trapped between sleep and wakefulness. She was vaguely aware of feeling depressed and defeated and very, very crabby. She was not at all willing to wake up. She buried her face in her pillow, determined to blot out the voice.

"Lexie!" it called.

She growled back without stirring or opening an eye.

"Lex, wake up." A hand gripped her shoulder.

She shook it off with another sound of protest, burying her face deeper into the pillow.

"Alexis, come on!" She was shaken again and turned over.

She flailed both arms to fend off the voice. She'd finally found solace in sleep and she wasn't giving it up.

"Go away!" she said clearly, loudly, still without opening her eyes.

"Now, how can I go away," the voice asked, a hand curling gently around her thigh, "when you love me so much?"

She surfaced from sleep with the power of an underwater missile.

She sat up in bed and found herself eye to eye with Trevyn, who sat beside her. His pleased smile was illuminated by the bedside light. He brushed the tumbled hair from her face, gently caught her neck in the circle of his hand and pulled her to him.

He kissed her slowly, deeply...*artistically*.

She succumbed to it for one treacherous moment, then slapped his hand away and fell back against the pillows, pulling the blankets up over her face. "I'm asleep!" she shouted through the layers of wool and down.

"Well, that's too bad," he said, "because I am—at long last—awake."

That sounded like a double entendre, but she was too smart to fall for it.

"Then go have some coffee," she said, "and let me be!"

His hand stroked her hip. She felt it as though there was nothing between his hand and her skin. She curled up against the sensation. No!

"I'm not going to make it without you," he persisted. "Come on. I have something to show you."

"I've seen it," she replied. "Very impressive. Now go away."

This time the hand swatted.

She yanked at her blankets and sat up again, fury heating her cheeks as she raised a hand to swing at him.

He caught her wrist and kissed her knuckles. There was amusement and a very unsettling adoration in his eyes. "What I wanted to show you," he said, with a quick scolding frown for her last remark, "was a dream I have."

The kiss on her fingers liquefied her spine, that look in his eyes making a puddle of her entire body. She had to make herself pull her hand away. "I was sleeping," she said, "and having my own dream. And anyway, I thought we'd decided that our dreams weren't compatible."

He shook his head. "I don't remember that."

She leaned her upper body toward him and glared

into his eyes. "'I don't want to go that deep,' means the same thing."

The sweet, self-satisfied expression disappeared and he looked suddenly penitent. "I'm sorry about that. That was stupid."

Alexis's heart slammed against her ribs, rose into her throat, then slipped back into place beating like a mad thing. No, no, no!

"Until you make love to me, then you'll change your mind again." She fell back against the pillows and turned away from him. "No, thank you."

IF HE WAS CONVINCED she meant that, Trevyn thought, studying the seductive curve of her back in a ruffly white muslin nightgown, he'd drive the Duesie off the cliff. But he remembered her portrait of him in the back room of his studio.

"I thought artists were adventurous," he challenged.

"I don't love you," she sat flatly without looking at him.

"Liar," he chided gently.

She sat up again, her hair a fiery riot around her head, her eyes red-rimmed from tears? Lack of sleep? "Is your ego so inflated that you can't believe I've gotten over you?"

He smiled sympathetically. That seemed to confuse her.

"No," he said. "But I've seen the painting."

She hadn't expected him to go to the studio today. That was clearly reflected in her horrified expression.

"I wanted to show my father the place," he explained. "We stopped by on the way home."

He could see in her eyes that she was desperately trying to regroup. "It makes no difference," she said calmly. "We've always known we love each other. We just decided not to act on it. When I tried to change my mind, you held to the plan. Now I'm doing it."

All right. She'd left him few alternatives. He stood and handed her the jacket he'd brought up for her from the closet downstairs. "Put this on," he said.

Her expression was dubious. "I'm not going anywhere." She dropped the jacket and folded her arms.

He didn't think arguing would get him anywhere, so he didn't try. He dropped the jacket on her shoulders, and when she lay back in an effort to thwart him, he knelt astride her and pushed her arms into the sleeves.

"What are you—? Don't you—! Trevyn!"

He pulled her to a sitting position, scooped her out of bed and headed down the hall with her, then down the back stairs that led to the kitchen.

The boys had apparently gone to bed, but David and Athena still sat at the table, chatting with Dotty. She had a laundry basket at her feet and was matching socks.

"Is she ill?" Athena demanded, getting to her feet.

"No, just stubborn," Trevyn replied. "I'm taking her out for a while."

"Would you two *do* something?" Alexis demanded, her arms folded, as he started toward the front of the house. "I don't want to go!"

"Trev!" David shouted.

Trevyn stopped and turned, prepared to defend his decision to override her unwillingness to cooperate.

But David simply grabbed a pair of slipper socks off the table and pushed them onto Alexis's feet.

"Thank you," Trevyn said.

David nodded. "Remember that she's my sister-in-law."

"Sure. I'm just trying to become your brother-in-law."

"Saints preserve us!"

"Trevyn McGinty, I wish to heaven I'd gotten you with that frying pan!" Lexie cried as David went before them and opened the front door. "And I'm going to get you, too, David!"

The door closed behind them and he stood her up in front of the Duesie's passenger door. She was too astonished at the sight of the car to struggle or consider escape.

"Where did this come from?" she asked.

"It's a gift from my father." He opened the door and helped her inside. "In honor of our engagement."

She shouted something at him, but he'd closed the door on her and was running around to the driver's side.

She glared at him as he started the motor, then didn't speak a word as they purred smoothly down the driveway and out onto the almost deserted highway.

ALEXIS COULDN'T BELIEVE this was happening to her.
Was she wearing some kind of sign that pleaded Kid-
nap Me! First the helicopter that had brought her to
Dancer's Beach, and now this!

And what had come over Trevyn? He didn't seem
to hear her when she said she didn't love him, didn't
want anything to do with him, didn't want to come
on this absurd middle-of-the-night adventure.

It was the painting. The cursed thing had been intended to purge her of him, and seemed instead to
have inspired Trevyn to finally allow her to love him.

Well, it would be February in hell before she admitted it.

He pulled the car to a stop in the cove, a quarter-
mile half-circle of sandy beach and houses tucked
away in trees on the far side of Dancer's Beach.

"Come on," he said. "You have to get out for the
best view."

"It's freezing," she said, pouting.

"I'll keep you warm," he promised, and opened
her door and scooped her up again. The air smelled
deliciously of salt water, pine and fall.

He walked with her across the sand to a spot where
a house stood on a little knoll on the near edge of the
cove's curve. All the downstairs windows were
brightly lit, one window showing light on the second
floor.

"You can't tell at night," he said reverently, "but
it's a craftsman's bungalow. Those are ash and fir
trees behind it with a couple of those shaggy pines
thrown in."

"It may have escaped you," she said gently, in deference to the emotions the place seemed to inspire in him, "but people are living in it."

He knelt on one knee in the sand and pulled her down onto the other. "I did notice that. But I walk by it a couple of times a week because it reminds me of the house I grew up in and I was a happy kid. It looks like it should be filled with happy kids, doesn't it?"

She was breathless, afraid to reply.

"Anyway, one day when I walked by, the man was painting the front porch and I asked him to call me if he was ever interested in selling. He said there was a possibility he might be transferred next year, and he took my name and number."

"And he's called you?"

"No. But all you have to do is tell me you love it as much as I do and I'll call him and see if we can make a deal."

They were surrounded by darkness, but for the first time in days she thought she saw the smallest glimmer of light. Her heartbeat accelerated and her breath caught.

She looked into his eyes, trying to read them and finding it difficult even though they were face-to-face. "You want to live with me in that house?" she asked.

He kissed her ear and leaned his forehead against her temple. "I want to be your husband in that house, the father of your children."

Light exploded, stunning her. Since he'd lifted her

off her bed, she'd been curled into a tight little ball of irritation and insecurity. But she felt herself unfolding like a flower with the light, looping an arm cautiously around his neck, drawing a deep breath.

He raised his head to look into her face. His chin was determined, but the expression in his eyes was watchful, uncertain.

"You want to get married." She had to make sure she wasn't delusional.

"Yes."

"To me."

"Yes."

"That's going pretty deep."

"I know. I'm finally ready." He tightened his grip on her. "I've lived with this dark place inside for so long. Then yesterday, I was trying to explain it to my father and I couldn't. You know why?"

"Why?" she whispered.

"Because it's gone. You know why?"

She swallowed. "Why?"

"Because you love me. And don't try to deny it, because it's all over that portrait of me." He uttered a little laugh that seemed to be more about surprise than mirth. "I just couldn't imagine that you could be happy with me until I looked into my face...as you see me."

BOTH HER ARMS CAME AROUND his neck and she dropped her head to his shoulder with a yielding sigh. "Trevyn. I like to think that tenderness in your eyes in the portrait is because you're looking into the love in mine.''

He said a silent prayer of gratitude that heaven had chosen to let him have what he truly didn't deserve. Mentally he squared up the past and put it away.

"I know this isn't the traditional scenario," he said with a light laugh, "but I am on one knee. Will you marry me?''

Her giggle surprised and touched him. She looked as though she might burst with happiness. "Yes!" she said firmly. "A thousand times, yes!''

There was no moonlight, no stars, just a cold October wind, but they held each other and kissed for a long, long time. Trevyn finally bundled her back into the car and drove home to Cliffside.

ATHENA, DAVID, MICHAEL and Dotty met them at the door, apparently feeling no qualms about expecting a full report.

It didn't seem to be required, however. When Trevyn put Alexis on her feet and she melted against his side, a ridiculously happy smile on her face, a collective cheer arose. There were hugs and congratulations, then Dotty ran to the kitchen for a bottle of champagne and glasses.

"When's the wedding?" Athena asked excitedly.

"When can you come back?" Alexis asked Michael.

Trevyn groaned. "Dad, I can't wait until Thanksgiving.''

Michael laughed, clearly delighted with the turn of events. "Maybe I'll just have to send the charity a big check and stay for the wedding."

Everyone endorsed that suggestion.

Alexis looked at Athena, her euphoria suddenly subdued. "God, I wish Gusty was here," she said.

Athena leaned over to pat her knee. "I know. We felt the same way."

"Lex said you have a list of the Shelldrake Inn registrations," David said to Trevyn. "Is it on you?"

Trevyn pulled the folded sheets out of his jacket pocket and handed them across the coffee table. David walked to the fireplace with them, perusing the list.

"I guess Lex told you we couldn't find anything on there to give us a clue."

Dotty returned with a tray bearing the bottle of champagne and six tulip glasses. She handed the bottle and a corkscrew to Trevyn, who opened it without mishap.

He was pouring the last glass when David uttered a sudden, crisp expletive. Trevyn put the bottle down and everyone else froze. "What?" he asked warily.

David came back to the group, pointing to the fourth reservation on the second sheet. "Mr. and Mrs. Jason Drake," he said. "That's a name Bram used on a job in Morocco."

Trevyn frowned. "I don't remember that."

"That's because it was a job he and I did together before you joined." David shook his head, a half smile on his lips. "No wonder no one can find Gusty. Bram's got her."

"But Athena told you on the phone that the police had the passenger lists' names narrowed down to Mr. and Mrs. Carter North. That didn't mean anything to you?"

David shook his head. "No. I suppose he could have made up an alias he's never used, or…"

"Or?" Alexis asked.

"The police are on the wrong track."

Alexis turned to Athena, then to Trevyn, unsure whether to be relieved or even more concerned.

Trevyn put an arm around her.

"Well, if she's with Bram, it means she's safe, doesn't it?" she asked anxiously.

Trevyn exchanged a look with David. "Unless *she's* done something to *him*."

* * * * *

Don't miss the conclusion
of Muriel Jensen's
WHO'S THE DADDY? *series!*

Coming next month,
Father Found!

Tyler Brides

It happened one weekend...

Quinn and Molly Spencer are delighted to accept three
bookings for their newly opened B&B, Breakfast Inn Bed,
located in America's favorite hometown, Tyler, Wisconsin.

But Gina Santori is anything but thrilled to discover her
best friend has tricked her into sharing a room with
the man who broke her heart eight years ago....

And Delia Mayhew can hardly believe that she's
gotten herself locked in the Breakfast Inn Bed
basement with the sexiest man in America.

Then there's Rebecca Salter. She's turned up at the
Inn in her wedding gown. Minus her groom.

*Come home to Tyler for three delightful novellas
by three of your favorite authors: Kristine Rolofson,
Heather MacAllister and Jacqueline Diamond.*

HARLEQUIN®
Makes any time special ™

Visit us at www.eHarlequin.com

PHTB

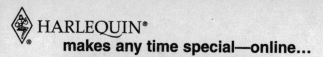

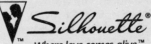

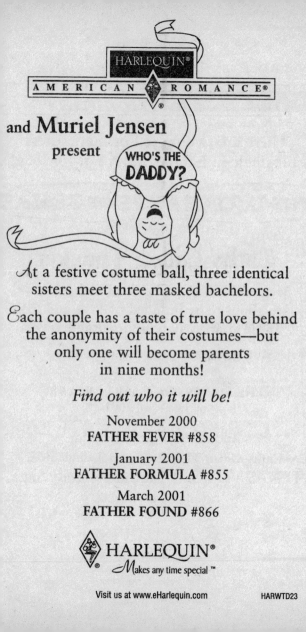

HARLEQUIN®

AMERICAN ◆ ROMANCE®

and **Muriel Jensen**

present

WHO'S THE DADDY?

*A*t a festive costume ball, three identical
sisters meet three masked bachelors.

*E*ach couple has a taste of true love behind
the anonymity of their costumes—but
only one will become parents
in nine months!

Find out who it will be!

November 2000
FATHER FEVER #858

January 2001
FATHER FORMULA #855

March 2001
FATHER FOUND #866

HARLEQUIN®
Makes any time special™